Here in the Night

Here in the Night

Stories

Rebecca Turkewitz

www.blacklawrence.com

Executive Editor: Diane Goettel
Book Design: Amy Freels
Cover Design: Zoe Norvell
Cover Art: "Ruin of a Georgian House" by Christopher Gee

ISBN: 978-1-62557-057-4

Published 2023 by Black Lawrence Press.
Printed in the United States.

The following stories have been previously published:

"At This Late Hour" in *The Masters Review*
"Search Party" in *SmokeLong Quarterly*
"The Attic" in *New South*
"The Nightmares of Jennifer Aiken, Age 29" in *Chicago Quarterly Review*
"Warnings" in *The Normal School*
"The Elevator Girl" in *LampLight Magazine*
"The Last Unmapped Places" in *Electric Literature's Recommended Reading*
"Sarah Lane's School for Girls" in *Bayou Magazine*
"Four Houses Down" in *Harpur Palate*

For my parents
with infinite gratitude

Contents

At This Late Hour

I've been working the front desk of the Leavitt Hotel for three years, but booking rooms and greeting guests is only part of my job. It took some persuading, but William, the owner, lets me haunt the place. When William hired me, the Leavitt was already considered one of the most haunted spots in New England. At first, William dismissed the spooky stories and the ghost-hunters' claims. He's a history buff, and he's been meticulously restoring the two-hundred-year-old mansion to as close to its original state as he can possibly make it. He couldn't see that hauntings and history are really just two sides of the same coin, just different ways of using what came before us to make sense of our lives. After a few months of gathering visitors' and staff members' accounts, I went to William with my proposal: I wanted to play up the hotel's ghostly reputation. I told him it could attract business, especially in the off-season when the summer beach-goers and the fall tourists have deserted us. I assured him I could draw in a crowd that would appreciate the original fireplace he had restored in the lobby and the antique light fixtures he was buying for the dining room.

To test the waters, William let me add a few eerie touches to the hotel website: a picture of the small graveyard on the northern side of the property and a black-and-white photo of the building with all the windows dark, save one. I left a few false reviews online, added some stories to ghost-hunting websites, and dimmed the lobby lights in the evening. When business picked up and guests started asking about the Leavitt family tree hanging on the lobby wall, William relented completely. Together, we installed new locks on the doors so I could present each guest with a heavy brass skeleton key. Once a month I give a ghost tour of the property, pointing out the spot in the yard where no grass grows, the empty stone well hidden behind a stand of birch trees, the unlit coal room in the basement, and the study where Samuel Leavitt supposedly died at his desk, still tallying the debts others owed him.

I've learned that the best way to cultivate spookiness is to only hint at it, letting the stories stand for themselves while I express my doubts. I tell people on my tours that I'm only the reporter. *The last guest just told me the craziest story as he was checking out,* I say as I hand over maps of hiking trails. Every now and then, when I'm feeling anxious or bored or the urge to pack up and move, I slip into empty rooms and leave handprints on the windows and mirrors or scurry noisily through the halls at night, rapping on the walls. At first, I didn't tell William about these last flourishes. But William spends hours trying to recover old tax records and photos, tracing the Leavitt-Johnson family tree, and scouring antique stores for rugs and furniture that match the original design of the house. He understands fascination with strange and particular things.

Blackstone, New Hampshire is a town that lends itself well to hauntings. Driving in on the main road, you pass the wide, hilly cemetery; the somber, spired churches; and the black clouds of flies swarming above the salt marshes. The town center is full of winding streets and old clapboard houses, and its crooked shoreline reaches, like a long arm, into the bay. Its nights are dark and full and brooding. It's the first place I've ever lived that has not lost its character or that excited feeling of newness, even with the dull slog of passing days. I came here from Manchester, leaving behind, at thirty-three, not much else besides a pervy boss at a waitressing job I hated, some friends who still occasionally forget I've moved away and text me about parties, and an apartment I shared with my ill-tempered ex-boyfriend.

Although I'm an avid collector of Blackstone's ghost stories and superstitions, I'm mostly skeptical when it comes to the occult. I'm sure the majority of the guests' accounts of sudden chills and wailing women aren't actually evidence of supernatural phenomena. But I love the stories and the way they grab hold of people and cast a spell over the hotel, giving shape to the night and its mysteries. And I don't doubt that people are sensing *something*—a shift in mood or change in the air. Why not entertain the idea that, for a few brief moments, the past can spread like a deep soft bruise into the present? How else can I explain the thrill I feel as I sit alone at the desk in the evening, hearing—or imagining I'm hearing—the rhythm of the ocean waves, even though we're almost a mile from the shore? And there is one ghost I do believe in. Everyone in Blackstone knows the legend of Emily Leavitt, and I feel her spirit, if not her actual specter, lingering.

Emily Leavitt's father, who made his fortune in shipping, was the original owner of the Leavitt estate. When Emily, his only daughter, fell in love with a sailor, he offered to pay the sailor to leave Blackstone. To Emily's horror, her beloved took the money and left. Emily spent a week in bed, refusing any food but bread and water. The next Sunday, Emily finally rose and dressed for church. After the service, when her family and the rest of the congregation were filing into the streets, Emily suddenly changed direction and raced through the throngs of people towards the rocky shoreline and hurled herself into the sea. The legend holds that on early winter mornings when it's just growing light you can hear Emily screaming as she plunges into the icy water. Especially susceptible young women might see Emily's form floating in the ocean, blue and shivering, beckoning for them to leap in and join her. The legend implies but does not say: *Don't ever join her*. The legend implies but does not say: *Watch your daughters closely*.

At the Leavitt, Emily's ghost has been sighted everywhere: pacing the halls at night, tapping at first floor windows, slamming attic and basement doors, breathing down the backs of guests' necks. Stormy nights, she wails with the wind over her lost love's betrayal. She breaks dishes. She peers through keyholes. She fights to be freed from locked rooms. She gives us something to whisper about when our shifts run long or our days get dull.

My first two years at the Leavitt were the calmest, most stable of my adult life. I was taking a long break from romance, trying to see if I could make my life feel steadier without the constant earthquakes of new relationships. The move to Blackstone was the first I'd made on my own, not following a boyfriend or a group of friends or taking some time to recuperate on my mother's couch. Sometimes I wonder why I wasn't lonely, but I felt at home, happy to wake up alone in my rented first-floor apartment with everything just as I had left it. So when Julie, a bartender in the hotel dining room, told me that she couldn't believe I hadn't noticed how much William wanted me, I was surprised to find how curious I was, how an old longing stretched inside of me and shook itself awake.

*

Several months ago, I took Julie to lunch at one of the seafood restaurants in town. She was having an uncharacteristic bout of self-doubt, worried about her looming college graduation and the formlessness of her future. Julie, a round-faced University of New Hampshire student with a low voice and a deep loud laugh that makes even strangers want to join in with her, reminds me of myself at her age: bored and restless, always certain that some undetermined future event will transform her life into something more interesting and worthwhile. The comparison makes me scared for her. I've tried to talk to her about it, but she always takes it the wrong way. She finds the comparison flattering. She says she hopes to stay as young as I seem, as if clerking at a hotel in my mid-thirties is something to strive for. She views my easy friendships with staff members ten or fifteen years my junior as proof of an ideal adult life. I warn her about my failed attempts at college, my debt, and the uneasy blur of my twenties, but she's unfazed.

I'd hoped to use our lunch to steer Julie through her crisis of confidence, but she was deflecting, telling me about her new relationship with her married American studies professor, whom she interchangeably referred to as Professor Danvers and Mathew. She was in the midst of complaining about his irrational jealousy at seeing her on campus with a male friend when William came over to our table, his face flushed, a small paper bag crushed in his hands.

"I think this is the first time I've seen you outside the hotel," he said to me. "I guess we both spend too much time there."

"Do you want to join us?" Julie asked.

"Oh, thank you, but I'm on my way to my mother's. I just saw you two in the window."

"Were you at the Book Barn?" I asked, nodding to the bag in his hands.

"I was. Actually, when I was there I found a book I thought you might like." He pulled out a collection of Victorian ghost stories. "I thought it might inspire you. You can consider it research, for the job."

I thanked him and told him I couldn't wait to get started on it. He left the restaurant, pausing in the doorway to wave at us.

"We always assumed he was gay and very discrete," Julie said. "But obviously he has quite the crush on you."

"I know I'm a favorite of his, but I don't think his interest is romantic. I don't think William does romantic."

"Are you kidding? Everyone's noticed. He never says no to you and he can't stop grinning whenever you're around. He even asks your opinion on designs for the hotel. From William, that's practically a marriage proposal."

"I hadn't thought about it. I guess I've never had a man who's interested in me just be *nice* to me."

"And he's old enough to be your father."

"Not quite, Julie. And you should talk."

"Please. Mathew is firmly located in hot older man territory. There's a difference between an *older man* and an *old man*."

I agreed that William was not the typical sexy older man type, but I did find him charming. I was certainly curious about him. At fifty, he'd never married, even though he is blandly handsome—sturdy and broad-shouldered with a shy smile and dark gray hair. His passions, if they can be considered passions, are strange but straightforward and he is unabashed about sharing them. He paints beautiful maps of the area and sells them in a tourist-trap gallery near the beach, and occasionally gives talks on local history at the public library. He used to be a lawyer, but now he spends his days fixing up the hotel, spending entire mornings on one room—painting the molding or repairing a spot of water damage in the ceiling. He lives in a small apartment on the first floor of the hotel with a bell rigged up so he can be on call if a guest needs something after the staff has gone home. He never complains and seems to want nothing he can't reliably and fairly easily obtain.

William often stopped by during my quiet weekday evening shifts, bringing me decaf coffee and books to borrow. We talked about his plans for the hotel or what I was reading. He told me about Blackstone's early maritime industries and I told him about unusual encounters with guests. Once, when I heard he was sick with the flu, I brought him chicken soup and read to him from a book of local legends I'd discovered in a used bookshop. I'd never thought of William's attention as anything more than an unlikely friendship. But under this new light, I re-examined the easy way we talked to one another. I could imagine going for walks in the woods on Sunday mornings, reading in front of the fireplace in William's living room during the long winter nights, asking each other if we wanted our coffee mugs re-heated when we let them grow cold. In spite of myself, excitement flickered in my chest—not quite like the nights when I would spot a cute stranger at a friend's party and feel the force of all the possibilities that might come from our meeting, but not entirely foreign from that sensation either.

*

The next few days I took more care with my makeup and spent more time picking out clothes. William didn't notice, but Julie did. She teased me about it relentlessly. She thought I was being cruel and enjoying the flattery of William's attention. She couldn't imagine I was actually considering dating him. But I was intrigued—I wondered what William's broad hands might feel like as they moved across my body.

"I find him interesting," I told Julie one night after her shift ended. "I know he's not the most exciting choice, but he's different from anyone else I've dated. He's the first person I can imagine growing old with. Actually, this is the first time in my life I can imagine myself getting old, at all."

"And that's a good thing?" Julie asked. She was sitting behind the desk with me, folding flyers for a whale watching tour into origami cranes. She kept checking her phone, so I knew the professor was supposed to have called her, probably hours ago.

"Yes," I said, with more confidence than I felt. "I think it's a good thing. But I wouldn't have when I was your age. And that's what got me into so much trouble."

"You don't strike me as someone who's done with trouble yet." Julie's phone buzzed and she dumped her cranes into the trash. "My ride's here," she said.

"Speaking of trouble."

She turned and grinned at me, the relief of finally hearing from the professor palpable in every gesture she made. She pulled on the hood of her coat and rushed outside. When she opened the door the loud static of rain and the smell of mud filled the lobby.

I hadn't realized how bad the storm was. I came out from behind the desk and went to the window. I watched the branches of the apple trees shimmying and listened to the shushing of the wet leaves. When I heard footsteps approaching, my breath caught and I froze. In the window's reflection, I saw William come around the corner holding a mug of tea. He looked behind the desk and then scanned the room. When his eyes fell on me he startled, and hot water splashed onto his hand. He dropped the mug and it cracked open.

"God," he said. "You really scared me. Your stories must be having some effect."

"I thought you said ghost stories were just easy entertainment."

"Everyone believes in ghosts when it's late enough. You're the one who taught me that."

"Ah. So you have been paying attention." I went to retrieve the pieces of the mug, then took his hand. I ran my thumb over the burn and William's arm began to shake.

"I doubt any guests are out in this downpour," William said. "You can take off for the night if you want to."

"I might wait for the rain to let up. I walked."

I was hoping he would offer to drive me home, but instead he suggested I stay at the hotel.

"There aren't any open rooms," I said. "We're full up."

"The couch in my living room pulls out," William said, and then flushed.

He waited for me to gather my things and we walked down the narrow hallways to his room.

His apartment was tidy and surprisingly modern compared to the museum-like quality of the rest of the hotel. I went over to his workbench and leaned over a sketch he was making of old shipping routes; several photocopies of charts were taped to the table.

"What is it about old maps that you find so fascinating?" I asked.

He ran a finger over the dark lines. "I don't know why I like them. Maybe that's why I don't get bored with them."

"You're trying to puzzle it out," I said. When he nodded, I told him about the times I had run through the hotel halls at night, doing Emily Leavitt's dirty work for her. William laughed, the wrinkles around his eyes deepening. I told him about standing on the lawn after midnight with my arms raised, hoping an insomniac guest would catch a glimpse of me, and how I left my handprints on glass surfaces.

"You leave handprints on the windows—in the guests' rooms?" William asked, suddenly serious, and I wondered if instead of sleeping with me he would fire me.

"Sometimes."

William sat down on the arm of the couch. "A friend of mine from law school stayed in room 304 in April. He said that he woke up in the middle of the night and saw a young woman rubbing a cloth against the windowpane, trying to clean what looked like fingerprints. When he started to cry out, he said the girl turned to him and shook her head as if she were scolding him, and then disappeared." William tugged at the cuff of his shirt. "It was just a dream, obviously, but Jim was so upset. He swore it was real. He made me promise not to tell anyone about it or mention it again. I've never seen him act like that."

I leaned against the workbench. "You're not teasing me?"

William shook his head. I moved to the couch and sat down. "It's probably just a coincidence," I said. But I was excited, even though the message was disconcerting if it was real. Some specter was warning me, saying, *Stop playing with these things you don't understand; watch yourself.* I looked up at William, who was still angled away from me.

"I should let you sleep," he said, standing up abruptly. "I'll get you a quilt. If you need anything, let me know."

I was so nonplussed I could only thank him. He was really going to leave me on the couch. Maybe I'd been mistaken about his interest, but I didn't think so. Once I had started looking for signs of his attraction, I'd seen them everywhere: in the moments he made eye contact and the moments he wouldn't meet my eyes, in the color that sometimes rose in his cheeks, in the little things he remembered about our past conversations. When he returned with a blanket and two pillows, he hesitated for one tense moment before retreating to his bedroom. I lay down but couldn't fall asleep. Around three in the morning the rain stopped, and the insects and night animals started stirring. A barred owl began to hoot, the sound low and mournful and questioning. It sounded like the call of an uncertain lover, saying, with its lilting tone, *Come to the window. Come to the window and throw me the key.*

*

I don't know when I fell asleep, but in my dream I could see much older versions of William and myself standing side by side behind the hotel desk. My face was pouchier and lined with wrinkles and my hair was silver, but I was dressed well and stood straight. The current version of myself watched the tableau, standing in a shadowed corner of the lobby. William put his hand on the small of the older me's back, and then pointed to the corner where I stood. The older me turned slowly and stared, before pulling her lips back to show her teeth. Every tooth in her mouth had been filed to a knife-like point. She kept her lips pulled back, not in a growl or snarl, but merely to show me. She snapped her teeth together twice, and I woke, slick with sweat, the covers pulled tightly around me.

I got up and opened the door to William's room. William was on his back, breathing through his mouth, his hair mussed. I pulled the covers away and slid towards his sturdy body. I put my hand on his chest and he opened his eyes.

"Oh, thank God," he said, taking my chin in his hand and kissing me. I was taken aback by how much he wanted me. He was careful, but also close to desperation. He was a hungry kisser, and I was relieved to find that I responded to him. His passion embarrassed me a little, reminding me that although I was attracted to him, it wasn't in the feverish way I was used to. I didn't feel overwhelmed or pulled underwater by ravenous tides.

At one point he stopped and said, "I'm sorry. It's been a long time since I've been with a woman."

"It's been a while for me, too," I said, but I knew we were using different scales to measure our abstinence.

Afterwards, as we lay on our backs holding hands, I asked him why he'd never been married.

"I almost was, once," he said. "I never really got up the nerve again. After a certain age, dating becomes mostly an embarrassing negotiation."

I laughed and turned to face him. "I'm just impressed you're willing to negotiate." I slipped my leg in-between his, and he kissed me in a way that was so grateful, I knew that if I wanted this, I could have it and probably have it for good.

*

The next day, I asked Julie to get drinks with me after work. Halfway to the bar, I realized Julie had already started drinking at the hotel. I assumed something had happened, either with her close-knit group of roommates or with the professor.

After Gayle, the bartender, had served us our drinks and updated us on her daughter's tricky pregnancy, I waited for Julie to explain what was bothering her.

"Did you know that Emily Leavitt didn't die when she threw herself into the water?" she said.

I shook my head. All the retellings I'd heard ended with Emily swallowed by rough seas or broken against the rocks.

"She bruised some ribs and got hypothermia, but she survived."

"I can't believe it. How'd you find out?"

"You're not the only one who reads," Julie said sharply, then took a breath. "I was curious. I went to the Blackstone library and found an article from the local paper about Emily's jump, which mentioned that she was recovering from the ordeal at home. Then I asked William for help. He did some digging and said there's almost no information about Emily's later life. But he found one reference to her being institutionalized a few years later."

"You asked William?" I said and Julie nodded. "What type of institution? An asylum?"

"William thinks she was hospitalized for typhoid fever, something about historical epidemics or whatever, but I think you're right. It must have been a mental asylum." Julie finished her drink and traced lines in the condensation on her glass. I'd never seen her in such a dark mood. I couldn't figure out if she was using Emily's story to stall or if she was trying to hint at something.

"Those *assholes*," Julie said without looking at me. "Maybe it would've been better if she had died that day. Gone out in a blaze of glory, sending the message she wanted to send."

"So Emily haunted The Leavitt even when she was still alive," I said. "She survived the jump, but she was already a ghost."

After Gayle brought us a second round, I told Julie what had happened with William, leaving out the awkwardness of the first part of the night spent on the couch.

"That's great," Julie said hollowly. "I mean, are you happy about it?"

"I think so," I said. "He's smart and honest and kind. I think maybe it's time I tried dating someone who cares about making me happy."

"And you love the hotel," Julie said, staring out the bar windows at the black stretch of water. "You *really* love this town."

"I do. But why does that matter?"

"No, I think this is a smart decision. Like you said, you can't just be a hotel clerk forever."

"That is not what this is about. What's got into you?"

"I've heard you talk about your past relationships. Even the men who were terrible to you. Don't pretend what you're feeling for William is the same kind of love."

"It's a relationship I can actually imagine lasting. That other kind of love never served me particularly well."

"But he really wants you. He's fallen *hard*."

"I'm fine with falling softly. I could use a little gentleness for once. You don't understand that yet, but you will."

Julie thumped her glass down on the bar, making the tonic in it hiss. "I understand *now*. I'm just honest with myself about what I want, and why."

"There's nothing wrong with figuring out how to make a life that's good for me. I'm sick of everything ending in disaster. And I don't know what you're angry about, but there's no reason to make me feel badly about William."

"I'm sorry. It's been a terrible night." Julie finished her drink and ordered another. "I know you think I don't care about any of the consequences of what I do."

"That's not what I think about you at all. Did Mathew break it off?"

"No," she said. "It's the opposite. He wants to leave his wife."

"For you?"

"You don't have to sound so surprised. But don't worry. I'm not going to let him."

"Let him? What if he just does it?"

"Then I'll leave him. I don't know why he assumes that's even what I want. The narcissistic asshole."

"I thought you wanted to be with him."

"He treats me pretty well. But, obviously, he treats his wife like shit. Who wants to be that person, boring and taken for granted? And what does Mathew expect? That I'll be some sort of stepmom to his kids, or dress up nice and hang on his arm at faculty events?"

Julie started crying. I knew she wasn't going to leave him, at least not for a while. I had been in her situation, or something like it, a few times before. She was upset because she'd go to the faculty events, meet his kids, learn what he was like when he wasn't trying to impress her, which would be all the time soon.

"Listen to me," I said, and Julie looked up. I wrapped my arm around her shoulders. "Please don't do this. Don't let him do this to you."

"I told you, I'm going to leave him."

She didn't believe that, I could see. She was repeating it like a mantra, the way you repeat 'there's no one there, there's no one there' when you hear a floorboard creak in the middle of the night. So I told her the real reason I had left Manchester and come to Blackstone, desperate for a place to settle.

One night, out with my coworkers, I had met a man who told me he was a musician. He asked if I wanted to go with him to see a band he knew play nearby. I didn't even tell my friends I was leaving, just let the musician drive me away from the city center, out towards the airport. After several turns away from the well-lit streets and onto roads flanked by woods, I began to panic. I was too drunk to figure out what to do or how to read his expression, which still seemed at ease. I couldn't focus. Even though I was flooded with adrenaline, I was so tired I had trouble keeping my eyes open. I wondered if he'd slipped me something. When he slowed at a stop sign, I flung the door open and raced into the trees. I don't know how he reacted because I never looked back. I wove as deeply into the woods as I could make it before my legs turned to jelly. I was sure the musician was somewhere in the darkness, stalking me. I passed out and woke at dawn. Somehow I found the road again and called one of my friends to come pick me up.

"I'm sorry," Julie said.

"I've had a lot of bad nights like that," I said. "I could have been killed. And for what? The possibility of a better party? I decided, right then, that I had to stop letting luck decide if I survived the day unscathed or not."

"Where's the fun in that?"

"I'm not kidding around. You see the 'me' that's made it to thirty-five, but in a dozen other branches of my almost-life, I'd be a cautionary tale. I've only told you about the times that make good stories. You don't want to hear about when I woke up with my roommate's fist in my mouth. I'd been choking on my own vomit in my sleep, too drunk to wake up or swallow. She was trying to claw the bile out of my throat."

"Gross," Julie said. Then, "I'm sorry."

"I was nineteen, and the very next night I had ten shots of whiskey and woke up in an ambulance. And that's just one example."

Julie studied the bubbles in her drink. "Have you told William about all that?"

I shook my head.

"And will you ever tell him about the night with the musician?"

"I might," I said, knowing I never would.

"That's what I thought."

We stayed out awhile longer, Julie sniffling her way through the rest of our conversation. Then I walked Julie back to my apartment and set her up on the couch, a blanket tucked around her. I considered the ways she'd been both right and wrong about William and me. I thought about whether it mattered how or even if I loved him, whether any of that trumped a settled, pleasant life.

*

I woke up to Julie standing in my bedroom doorway, her shoulders moving up and down as she sobbed. I scrambled out of bed and pulled her into a hug. She was soaking wet and freezing.

"What the hell happened to you?" I asked. "Are you all right?"

Julie kept crying, and I pushed her sopping hair away from her face. Her teeth were chattering. There was a scrape on her elbow, and the blood had thinned and spread across the wet surface of her arm.

"I jumped in," Julie said.

"In where?"

"Just to see what it was like," she said.

"Not into the ocean?" I asked, and Julie nodded.

"I'm so cold."

It was almost dawn and I could hear the birds waking up outside. I took her into my bathroom and stuck her under the shower, rubbing her arms. I kept repeating, "You're okay, you're okay."

She changed into dry clothing while I made tea. Her eyes were unfocused and she was still drunk, but I could see her head was clearing.

"Jules," I said, trying to sound comforting and not reproachful. "Why did you jump?"

"I wasn't trying to hurt myself, if that's what you mean. I just went for a walk and I thought, why not?"

"Have you ever tried anything like this before?"

"I wasn't trying to *hurt* myself," she said. "I swear."

"You just thought, 'Gee, why don't I go for a five a.m. swim in the open ocean?'"

"You don't remember what it's like. Not anymore," Julie said.

But that wasn't true. Of course I remembered: the hot fist of need nestled in my stomach, the longing sharp and pressing but without aim, the desire to quench it in any way possible.

"You're going to be okay," I said. She fell asleep with her head in my lap.

*

Later that morning, Julie and I went to breakfast in town and the waitress told us the latest gossip. Bill Patterson, the owner of Patterson's Clams, had seen a young woman leap off the seawall as he was getting dressed. He ran outside and down to the water, but never saw anyone surface. Soon, the story was all over town. Most people speculated that Bill had been fooled by some trick of the pre-dawn light. Quite a few locals insisted he'd seen the apparition of Emily Leavitt. Julie and I didn't tell anyone what had really happened. We let the story spread and work its way into the town lore. We let Emily's ghost have a little more life.

That afternoon, Julie seemed in better spirits. We laughed about what would have happened if Bill had been a little quicker and come upon Julie clambering out of the water, smelling like gin. Every hotel staff member wanted to be the first to tell us about Bill's sighting, and we smiled mysteriously whenever anyone asked what was so funny. But the next day, Julie pulled me aside and told me that she wondered if Emily had been involved after all. She showed me a purple bruise that had bloomed on her upper arm. Four welts extended from it like the imprints of strong fingers. Julie's face was pale and I asked if she'd slept. She shook off my question and said she couldn't remember why she'd wandered down to the water in the first place. The spot she jumped from wasn't particularly high, but it was rocky. People have died from less. Julie told me she sometimes dreams of a girl calling to her. She knows she shouldn't follow the voice, but she always does. "Maybe this time I just didn't wake up before I found her," she said.

*

To know a place, you have to know its ghosts. As with people, you need to understand the particular ways in which towns are haunted before you can understand them. Emily has worked her way into Blackstone's makeup. She walks this town's streets and controls its tides. I see her in the faces of the college girls who come for a summer weekend, their hair heavy with saltwater, their eyes trained on the white-capped waves. I see her in the women wearing too-thin jackets on October afternoons, holding their partners' hands so tightly that their knuckles are bloodless and pale. I hear her in the low humming of night insects; I feel her breath in the late-August air. Here, Emily follows behind me like a big black dog, saying, *Come back to me, turn around and look at me, answer me when I call.* And I like to keep her around as a reminder. She's also saying, *Careful of this thing that lives inside you.* When the hotel staff trade stories about waking up in unusual places or taking pills that strangers give them in public restrooms, I tell myself, 'I used to live that way and now I don't.' I've stopped the spinning wheels of disaster and laid claim to my own life.

When I stay over at William's, I feel Emily watching from outside the window, trying to make sense of my happiness and the steady, sure comfort that comes from lying next to William. She wants to draw me back into her world, to remind me what it's like to return a stranger's smile or feel the night hanging ahead of me, open and unplanned like an empty road. I will not be convinced, but still I conjure her. I cannot bear to lay her to rest. Julie occasionally jokes with me about Emily—she says I've strayed from Emily's teachings about rash decisions and life choices my parents would disapprove of—but I've noticed Julie won't go into the basement or the pantries alone anymore. She tells me less and less about the inner workings of her life and makes excuses when I ask her to go on evening walks down to the shore. She still hasn't left her professor, and he almost always picks her up after her late shifts.

William often talks about what a miracle it is that we found each other. He says it's a wonder that two people who are so superficially different but share so much came together at just the right point in our lives. It amazes him that we feel the same thing for one another at the same time, as if mysterious currents have carried us together at random. I murmur my agreement, but I am done with currents. I have put my anchor down.

Search Party

Richard had bought me hot chocolate and churros, which was the kind of thing he always did when he felt guilty. The texture of the hot chocolate was like sludge and I imagined my stomach filling with mud. I pushed it away.

"Eat, beautiful. Please. Do you want something else?"

I shook my head. My hair was uneven and shorn up to my ears. I'd hacked it off the week before with nail scissors in a hostel bathroom in Lisbon while a backpacker—a white kid with blond dreadlocks and duct-taped shoes—watched warily. 'How old are you?' he'd asked. 'Sixteen,' I'd told him, though I was really fifteen. He gestured towards the locks of wet hair on the ground and said, 'Bold look. I'm into it.' I told his reflection, 'I didn't do it for you.' The kid laughed. 'I bet you did it to piss off your old man.' 'He's my step-father,' I said. The kid had held up his calloused hands defensively and said, 'My bad.'

A few days after that, Richard moved us on to this tiny town in the mountains of Spain, where there were sheep dotting the hillsides and centuries-old stone archways. Our hotel—a small guesthouse—was in the main square and every hour the church bell clanged so loudly I could feel it in my teeth. The people mostly spoke Basque, so the little Spanish I knew was useless when I tried to eavesdrop. In a week we'd be back home, and the mercy of school would start, and there'd be friends' houses to stay over at and books to get lost in and new teachers to gossip about. Not just Richard filling every space.

When the waitress returned, Richard ordered croissants and fresh-squeezed juice. "You're getting too thin," he said.

"I'm not hungry."

"Look, I'm sorry," he said. "But don't you like it here?"

I clenched my jaw and turned away. It was the most beautiful place I'd ever been. The clouds hung low overhead and the air was crisp and fragrant, as if it had always just stopped raining. The buildings, with their bursting window boxes and brick-colored roofs, leaned into one another. Tiny black birds shaped like arrows dove into the river below.

On the patio, a couple at the next table over was watching us and whispering. I thought maybe they were disapproving of my hair, or the safety pins in my ears, or my surliness. I imagined their disdain: *Americans! They can't even control their children. Who lets a girl walk around looking like that?*

"We can go home," he said. "If that's what you want, I can move our flight up."

"Can we?" I asked, and Richard looked wounded.

He sighed. "Yes. Okay. For you, you know I would do anything." He gestured for the check.

The waitress came over and, with a flurry of apologies, told us we'd have to wait. Richard didn't understand, but shrugged. He was very easy-going. I'd heard other people call him *kind-hearted, a big softie*. I nudged my churro off the plate, then let it roll off the table. The waitress studied my face until I lowered my eyes. She disappeared inside.

When she returned, two policemen were with her. Their English was not good. We knew they wanted our passports, but couldn't see why. Eventually, they pulled the hotel manager over to translate. He looked painfully embarrassed. It took him several minutes to explain, to say *Beth Waters*.

I recognized the name instantly. Beth was a dark-haired, doll-faced American girl with plump cheeks and long eyelashes. She'd gone missing from her locked hotel room in Portugal two weeks ago. She was twelve years old. Her photo was on every news channel, followed by flashing numbers to call to report a sighting. Someone had spotted Richard and me and thought I might be Beth, after a hasty haircut and two weeks of malnourishment. "I'm not her," I said. "My name's Marigold. I'm *fifteen.*"

"I know," the hotel manager said, his blush moving all the way up his bald head. "I know, that's what I tell them. I tell them it's not true." He looked at Richard, "I'm so sorry, to you and your lovely daughter."

"Step-daughter," I said.

"It's all right, Miguel," Richard said. "They're only doing their jobs. It's better to be safe."

Richard went to get our passports. The couple that'd been whispering had left, and I wondered if they'd been the ones who reported us. Their spent plates were still on the table, lipstick staining one of the cups. What had they seen when they looked at us? What did they see that my friends' parents, that my grandmother, that our friendly neighbors couldn't see? That even my mother, when she was still alive, hadn't seen.

I noticed a paper in one of the police officer's hands. I reached for it and he gave it to me. He knew, by then, that they had the wrong girl. I laid out the flyer and looked into Beth's dark almond-shaped eyes. We did look a little alike, if she'd been thinner and angrier. In big letters, it said, "DESAPARECIDA." A small mean part of me hoped they'd never find her, though I assumed they would. There was an entire continent of people following her story, calling in tip after tip. I hated her sweet gap-toothed smile. I hated everyone trying so desperately to rescue her.

How could I have known they wouldn't find her? If I'd known, I'm sure I would've had kinder thoughts.

Richard came back and handed over the passports, wheezing slightly. "I'm sorry," he told the officers. He was always apologizing. He rested his wide palm on my shoulder.

I held my breath while the officers scanned my photograph and then checked my face.

But what could they see there? No one was looking for me.

The Attic

Anne and Kayla are supposed to be packing up the contents of Anne's attic. Instead, they're sifting through Anne's parents' possessions in search of something scandalous and exchanging secrets of their own. In one week, Anne will move 700 miles away from this small Massachusetts town where she's lived almost her entire life. The thought of moving makes her chest feel too full, as if something scratchy and fat has taken up residence beneath her ribcage, so she tries not to think about the move at all. Normally, Anne dislikes being in the attic. She hates its shadowed corners, its dusty smell, and the thick, hot air. But with Kayla sitting so near, Anne's enjoying herself. She had used the attic's creepiness to entice Kayla into joining her in packing, exploiting Kayla's love of the unusual. Anne had told Kayla that she thought the attic was haunted, even though Anne doesn't believe in ghosts.

"You're being quiet again," Kayla says. She has arranged some of Anne's old stuffed animals, which they found in a box labeled 'Anne's Pets,' to form a wide circle around herself. She's lying in the middle of it, her long brown hair wound into a coil beneath her head.

"I'm just thinking."

"I've been waiting for you to say something for five whole minutes and you've just been sitting there. You're such a weirdo."

"I know I am. But you like weird things."

"I do," Kayla acknowledges.

In the world of fifteen-year-olds, theirs is a miraculous friendship. Anne doesn't have many friends, and the ones she does have she rarely sees outside of school or art club. Kayla has many friends—happy, pretty friends who have boyfriends with names like Chad or Christian or Jeff. Kayla's at the very top of the social hierarchy. She's untouchable—cool even though she does bizarre things like form friendships with quiet weirdos like Anne.

"I hope you've been thinking about a deep, dark family secret," Kayla says. "Because it's your turn."

"I'm afraid of spiders," Anne says. "When I see one I panic."

"Nobody likes spiders. I want a *real* secret."

"I saw a therapist for it," Anne insists. But Kayla isn't satisfied, so Anne continues to think. Anne hadn't understood how the girls at her school could spend so much time doing nothing—talking on the phone, chatting in coffee shops, giggling at sleepovers. But now Anne sees how you can spin whole hours of nothing into something tangible and mesmerizing. It's a type of alchemy; it's a new and magnificent language she's becoming fluent in. She briefly considers telling Kayla about the mornings when she wakes up before school too afraid to get out of bed, paralyzed by the thought of all the stupid or offensive things she might accidentally say or have said to her. But she suspects this is probably too much, too soon. Instead she says, "When I was younger, when I had my head pressed against my pillow at night, I thought the sound of my own heartbeat was the sound of a man shoveling underneath my bed, digging his way towards me."

"But your room is on the second floor," Kayla says, her voice tinged with pleasure.

"I thought he was way far down in the earth. Digging his way through the soil. And I could hear him through the foundation of the house."

Kayla sits up. A strand of her hair gets caught on a nail in the floorboard and she winces. "Do you think it has anything to do with your adoption?" she asks. "A man digging his way from Korea to take you back. Digging from the other side of the world?"

"No. I don't think it had anything to do with that."

Kayla always wants to talk about the adoption. She wants to know how it feels for Anne to have white parents or if she finds it frustrating to live in a mostly white town or if she wants to meet her birth parents.

"It's your turn," Anne says.

Kayla tells Anne about the time she stayed after school to ask Mr. Levine about a bad grade on an algebra exam and found him stroking himself over his pants. "He was just sitting there at his desk," Kayla says, scrunching up her nose. "Not even really looking at anything. Just doing it absent-mindedly, staring off into space."

"What did you do?" Anne asks.

"Nothing. He stopped when he saw me standing there. His face turned bright red. And then he helped me with my math test."

"I would've been mortified. I would have run away."

"But *I* didn't have anything to be ashamed of." In the washed-out attic light Kayla looks especially beautiful. Her eyelashes make shadows on her cheeks like little cats' claws.

"I have a really good one. One I haven't told anyone before," Anne says. A shiver of anticipation flickers down her spine. "I didn't speak until I was almost four. For two years after I was adopted, I was totally silent."

"Why?"

"Nobody knows. My parents freaked out, and they took me to speech therapists and psychologists. I could understand other people perfectly well, but I wouldn't say anything. If I wanted something, I would draw it or act it out. And when I started speaking, I spoke in full sentences, without any baby talk."

"What was the first thing you said?" Kayla asks.

"'I'm hungry.' It nearly scared my mom to death. She says it was eerie, to hear my voice after so long. And it was strange that I sounded like a regular person suddenly."

"And no one knows why. They never figured it out?"

"The psychologists thought it was due to some early traumatic experience. The place my parents adopted me from didn't know what happened to me before I arrived there, when I was one. My parents think something terrible happened to me."

Kayla breaks through the circle of stuffed animals and scoots next to Anne. "That's awful. You poor thing." She links her arm through Anne's. "You never cease to surprise me."

Anne's parents still believe something horrific happened—the kind of thing you see specials about on *60 Minutes*—but Anne doesn't think anything extraordinary or awful happened to her. Anne believes that she was just never normal and, even from birth, she was slower than most at learning how to navigate the world.

"I can't imagine what that must be like," Kayla says. "To have the beginning of my life be a total mystery. Maybe the most important thing that ever happened to you, and you don't even know what it is. What do *you* think?"

"I don't want to know," Anne says, pulling closer to Kayla.

In the big open space of the attic, Anne feels a peculiar hum of electricity passing around them. Ever since they were seated next to each other in their fourth period art class, Anne has loved Kayla. Anne's feelings were at first only a dull, tingling ache, which could've easily been interpreted as admiration, or envy, or excitement at the prospect of a new friend. But now with the dread of the move and the eerie spell of the attic, Anne's love has become larger, something outside of herself that she must acknowledge. She shivers and their elbows knock together.

"Are you okay?" Kayla asks. "What's wrong?"

"Nothing. The attic is just spooky. I felt like someone was watching us."

"Oh yeah. *Definitely* haunted."

"You think so?"

"Absolutely," Kayla says, grinning. "It's haunted by the spirit of a girl who died here. Falling from the attic window, maybe?" She takes Anne's hand in her own, and rests it on her leg.

"Oh, come on." Anne wants to say something more, but she's too focused on the way her hand feels on the bare skin of Kayla's calf, which is prickly with recently shaved leg hair.

"The girl lived here with her parents a hundred years ago. They were the first people to live in the house. She was thirteen when she died. She was a weirdo, like you. Very quiet all the time." Kayla shakes Anne's arm playfully. "She had psychic powers. That's why she's still here."

Anne laughs and pulls closer to Kayla. "You're making me nervous. How do you come up with this stuff?"

"I'm not coming up with it. She's really here. You said you felt her watching you."

"Not *her*, or anyone, just a general vibe."

"I can sense her. Where do you think that feeling comes from?"

"I don't know. Attics are creepy. Do you really believe in ghosts?"

"Of course. What's her name, do you think?"

Anne listens to the attic noises: the house settling, the neighbor's air conditioners, the whine of the old light bulb. She imagines she's listening for a little girl to whisper a name. "Hazel," she says.

"Hazel," Kayla repeats, trying it out. "Because she was born with hazel eyes."

"Her eyes glowed when she was happy," Anne says. "Or scared."

"Or hangry." Kayla laughs.

"Her parents didn't know what to make of her."

"That's right." Kayla drops her chin to her freckled shoulder and lowers her voice. "Since she could make strange things *happen*."

Small things at first: the door to her room creaking open when she called out at night and no one came; books falling from the shelves when she bumped her knee; flickers of lamplight when her mother tickled her feet. Anne loses track of who supplies each new detail. She feels the story taking shape around them.

At first Hazel's parents tried to ignore the signs, worrying privately at night. Then they made jokes about the incidents, pretending they didn't believe but acknowledging the mysterious coincidences. Whenever the wind would gust during Hazel's restless moods they'd say, 'Turn off the storm, sweetheart.' Or when they wanted rain for the garden, they'd joke, 'Let's hope Hazel cries soon.'

"I like that," Kayla says. "It feels true. I think maybe Hazel's come out from hiding."

"Cut it out. You're scaring me." Anne's wrist itches, but she doesn't dare move to scratch it. Their hands are still joined, a thin layer of sweat sandwiched between their palms. Anne has to admit that the story seems to have come from somewhere outside of herself. The details came as if she were discovering them instead of inventing them. She can picture Hazel vividly: long black hair; skin the color of an apple's flesh; a blue, collared dress with a stiff skirt; small hands and high cheekbones; eyes with big dark pupils.

Neighborhood children are playing in a yard nearby and the flutter of their laughter enters the attic.

"Do you hear that?" Kayla asks.

"The kids?"

"No. If you're quiet you can hear Hazel breathing."

Anne listens obediently to the patterns of her and Kayla's breath. Her own breath is quick and shallow; Kayla's is slow and soft. But Anne also senses something extra—something formless, but heavy and real.

Anne turns to Kayla, who takes Anne's chin in her hand and pulls their faces together. Anne is so surprised by the kiss that she doesn't react and it's over before she can respond. It's her first. She hopes that Kayla will kiss her again so Anne can at least try to do more than bump lips. Kayla looks pleased with herself, but for once she's quiet and waiting.

Anne leans into Kayla awkwardly, and they kiss again. Their mouths fit together better than Anne imagined mouths could. Kayla moves her lips gently and expertly, reminding Anne that Kayla has done this before. This is a scratch at the side of her happiness, but Anne tries to push it aside.

After some time, she doesn't know how long, Anne hears her mom padding down the hallway below, and then footsteps on the attic stairs.

Anne straightens up and untangles herself from Kayla.

Her mother appears in the doorway and takes in the attic's disarray and the stuffed animals splayed out on the floor. "I see you girls didn't get much done," she says. "It's time for me to take Kayla home." Anne expects her to be annoyed at their lack of progress, but her mother only says, "I guess you two'll have to keep at it tomorrow."

But Kayla can't come tomorrow. Tomorrow Kayla's going to the pool with Jenna and Libby. Which of course makes sense; Kayla has other friends with whom she can participate in normal fifteen-year-old-girl activities.

"Don't worry," Kayla says. "I'll help you pack on Thursday."

Anne wants to say that she can't wait that long and even a day without Kayla will be torture. Instead she nods. "Thursday's great."

*

That night, in the swampy July heat, Anne can't sleep. She imagines all the places Hazel might be hiding: Hazel peering out of the closet; Hazel perched on the foot of the bed; the folds of Hazel's skirt rustling past Anne's slightly ajar bedroom door; Hazel still trapped in the attic with her ear pressed to the floorboards, listening to the sounds of Anne's sleep. In between these bouts of terror, Anne tried to remember every detail of their kissing. She finds it remarkable how similarly she feels physically when she recalls the kisses and the ghost story. Both memories elicit a frenzied, irrepressible response, like something throwing itself against the walls of her stomach and chest. When she pulls the sheet over her head to protect her neck, she hears the rapid-fire beating of her heart. Although it's been years since she's been afraid of her underground tunneling man, the thumping still makes Anne think of digging.

Does Kayla love her, Anne wonders. Had Kayla ever kissed another girl, or only the boys that Anne has heard about? What does Kayla—bold, smart, untouchable—find interesting in Anne—small, twitchy, nervous? Kayla is most likely interpreting Anne's quietness as a sign of depth or mystery. How long before Kayla realizes that Anne is not proudly weird, but anxious to be normal? Anne yearns for blankness, for a settled, calm quiet to fall over her. She tries to recall all the lyrics of songs she likes, the few ones that aren't about love.

She has just slipped into a daze resembling sleep when she hears someone passing through the hallway outside her room. Anne's whole body stiffens and seizes up, until the footfalls reach the stairs and their quick, clopping pattern becomes familiar. Her mother.

Anne's mother is frequently up at this hour, unable to sleep and restless. It has always seemed like an uncharacteristic habit for a woman who Anne thinks of as sturdy and unflappable. But Anne has woken many nights to the sound of her mother moving through the hallway and then microwaving hot water for tea. Anne slips out of bed. When she passes by the door that leads to the attic she feels a puff of hot air, as if the attic has just exhaled. Anne takes the stairs two at a time. Her mother is at the table in nothing but her underwear and a long t-shirt, sketching an elaborate design on a pad of paper. She looks surprised but not startled.

"What are you doing awake?" she asks.

"I couldn't sleep." Anne sits down in the chair kitty-corner to her mother. "Mom, I don't want to move."

"I know," her mother says with a sigh. "You're hard to read sometimes, but not that hard."

"I don't want to start at a new school. I like it here."

"I know it seems scary, but maybe it will be good for you to start over."

"I didn't say I was scared," Anne says. "I just don't want to go. You never asked me if I wanted to move."

"We don't really have a choice at this point, Annie. It's a better job for your dad, and it's where the company needs him."

"He could find a new job. Here."

"It isn't quite that simple." Anne's mother puts a hand on Anne's wrist. She does administrative work at a hospital and when she gets this close to Anne, Anne often catches a whiff of hospital sanitizer. Anne associates the smell with sickness and contagion instead of cleanliness. "I think the move might be good for you. You'll meet new people, and maybe it will be easier than you think to make friends if you're starting over."

"I don't want new friends. I don't want to live in a city I've never been to." Anne has only been to the Midwest once, on a trip to Cold Springs, Indiana for a cousin's wedding. She remembers the nighttime drive back to the airport and the shadowed fields that stretched outward from the road until they faded into nothing. She remembers feeling exposed.

"I'm sorry, sweetheart. But you should try to think of some of the good parts of moving. You might be surprised."

"Don't talk to me like I'm a four-year-old," Anne says.

Her mother rubs her eyes with the bases of her palms, her fingers splayed open in frustration. "I don't know what to say to you. We're leaving in a *week*."

"You always claim you want me to tell you what I'm thinking, but when I do you don't want to hear it. It doesn't make any difference how I feel—you just ignore me."

"I'm glad you're telling me," her mother says. "Really, I am."

"Let's stay here then. I don't want to have to start over."

"And you think I do?" her mother says, her voice cracking. "Do you really think that *I* do?" Without warning, her mother begins to cry. "I'm just tired," she says. "I'm sorry."

Anne stands up, unsure of what to do next, and then places her hand on her mother's shoulder. Her mom looks frail in the stark kitchen light, the spaces under her eyes thrown into shadow, her veiny thighs sticking out from under her nightshirt.

Two years ago, Anne's aunt, drunk on red wine at Passover, had told Anne about her mother's three failed pregnancies—the ones that had presumably led her parents to adopt. She and her aunt had been washing dishes in the kitchen while the rest of the family chatted in the living room. Her aunt had gotten teary, telling Anne about how brave and broken-hearted her good mother had been. One of the pregnancies had even come to term; her mother had gone through eight hours of labor and the baby was born tinted blue. Anne had never asked her parents about this and they'd never brought it up with her. But Anne thinks of these three babies often, especially of the stillborn one. She wonders if her mother held the body and what the child must have looked like. Anne imagines a delicate shade of lavender-blue. She wonders, too, if this is what her mother dwells on during her nighttime wakefulness.

When her mother composes herself, they share a clumsy hug. Her mother laughs. "I don't know what brought that on," she says. They walk upstairs together in solemn single file. Anne gets into bed, but doesn't turn off her light. "We're both going to be fine," her mother says softly. "I hope you know that."

Anne wishes she had pressed her mother further. Just like that, the conversation had ended, and now Anne is no closer to getting what she wants. Her mother is no closer to understanding how she feels. Anne is half an hour closer to the move and losing Kayla forever.

She rolls over in bed to check the time on her phone and finds a text from Kayla saying that Kayla can't sleep. Anne slips out of bed to shut the door, and dials Kayla's number.

Kayla answers after three rings.

"Were you thinking about Hazel?" Anne asks.

"No, silly. I was thinking about you."

Anne doesn't know how to respond.

"And okay, fine, also Hazel," Kayla says. Her voice is low and muted. She must be lying with her face against the phone.

"I've been thinking about Hazel, too."

"Tell me more about her," Kayla says. "Any more *discoveries*?"

Anne considers for a moment, staring out her window at the big maple tree in the yard. When Hazel turned twelve, Anne explains, the fires began. Little fires in the walls where there was no wiring. A bush in flames when no one was in the yard. Her father finding the curtains in her bedroom singed when he went to wake her from a fitful sleep. The neighbors began to wonder about the quiet, intense girl with the deep-set eyes. They noticed the way the noise of crickets would stop when she walked down the street at dusk.

Then, one evening, her mother sent Hazel to bed without dinner for losing her temper with her baby brother, and the bathroom mirror exploded into shards as Hazel walked by. Her parents became afraid of Hazel and her unpredictable moods. Although she insisted she wasn't doing anything on purpose, they didn't like the wild look in her eyes when she was upset, or her long hours of unbroken silence, or the brooding restlessness she'd often fall into when she was bored. They began to lock her in the attic.

"That seems cruel," Kayla murmurs, her voice on the edge of sleep.

"They didn't know what else to do."

"I don't think I've ever heard you talk for this long all at once," Kayla says. "Keep going."

Towards the end of Hazel's life, she spent more and more of her days locked in the attic. She became moodier, angrier, and unsettled, which made the fires worse. During a storm, a bolt of lightning struck the fence in the backyard. The smoldering wood sent waves of smoke towards the house.

Anne can picture the scene. The way the black smoke would obscure the one small window. The attic, at that time not wired for electricity, would have fallen into darkness. Hazel would have felt so alone. But not scared. She did not scare easily.

"Anne? Are you still there?" Kayla asks. "You should come with me tomorrow. To the pool, with Libby and Jenna."

"I don't think they like me."

"Of course they do. And I want to see you. And even better if it's in a bathing suit."

"Okay, I'll come."

After they hang up, Anne doesn't fall asleep until dawn.

*

When Anne's mom drops her at the pool, Kayla has to come outside to sign Anne in as a guest. Kayla's hair is damp.

"Have you been here awhile?" Anne asks, straining to peer into the parking lot so she can be sure her mom has left. She reaches for Kayla's hand.

"We've been here for a bit." Kayla takes her hand back. "I didn't tell Jenna or Libby that there was anything going on with us. So, you know?"

"Okay."

"Don't give me that face." Kayla pinches Anne's side. "You're not the one who'll have to face the rumors at our idiotic school in September."

The pool is bright and crowded. Jenna and Libby lounge in plastic chairs, their pale legs stretched out and crossed at the ankles. Kayla plops down on the edge of Jenna's seat, leaving a chair open for Anne. Anne sits and considers whether she should strip down to her bathing suit. The tableau that the three other girls form is like a movie poster: smooth stomachs, bright smiles, and a command of their bodies that Anne finds baffling.

Anne focuses on trying to hide the sweat stains spreading over her t-shirt while the girls talk about summer plans, friends that Anne barely knows, beach trips they went on last year, and the pros and cons of not being back at school for another two months. Anne becomes interested when the girls start talking about how Jenna's boyfriend thinks Jenna is still a virgin. When she notices Anne's piqued interest, Jenna cuts Libby off abruptly.

"Oh. I'm not going to tell anyone," Anne says quickly. "And I don't think it's a bad thing. I mean, I think it's fine. If you're worried about that."

Jenna laughs, and swipes her hand at the air. "Relax. I wasn't accusing you of anything. You were just so quiet, I practically forgot you were here."

"That happens a lot," Anne says. The other girls laugh, even Kayla, who must know Anne wasn't trying to be funny.

Jenna leans in towards Anne. "We heard about your adoption, and the not speaking. That is so crazy."

Anne must look panicked, because Jenna tries to backtrack. "Not crazy in a, you know, a literally crazy way. Crazy as in interesting. Kind of cool. I'd be dying to know what happened to me."

Anne wants to be back in the dark quiet of the attic, watching the world through the thick glass of the attic window. She wants to be alone again, with her secrets kept to herself.

"It wasn't a big deal," Anne says, because everyone is looking at her. It's probably been too long since she last spoke. What would Hazel do? The sickly-smelling pool water would start to churn, would rise up and swallow them all.

"Did Kayla tell you about *everything* that happened yesterday?" Anne asks.

Jenna and Libby turn to Kayla, who looks—for maybe the first time since Anne has known her—flustered.

Anne draws the silence out. Then, "We saw a ghost."

"Oh, really?" Jenna asks, her eyebrow raised. "You saw a ghost, Kayla?"

Kayla says, "Not a real ghost. We were just kidding around. Her attic is unbelievably creepy. You guys should see it."

"She *was* a real ghost," Anne says. "Kayla thought so, at least."

Kayla laughs too loudly. "That's why I love hanging out with her. She believes *everything*. It's great."

"I need to go home," Anne says, already out of her chair. "To finish packing."

Kayla calls out to her as Anne walks across the hot concrete, but none of the girls get up to follow. Anne can feel the force of Jenna and Libby's confusion. She hears one of them ask, "What's wrong with her?"

She pauses long enough to hear Kayla's response. "Who knows? She has issues."

When Anne calls her mom for a ride from the parking lot, her mom asks if she's okay.

"I don't feel well," Anne says, which isn't a lie.

*

Anne ignores Kayla's calls and apology texts for two days before finally relenting and inviting Kayla over. The two days had passed in a sleepless, hazy blur. Nights, Anne had stayed up thinking of Hazel. She created new layers of the storyline, imagining times that Hazel had run away from home. In the mornings, Anne had gone on long walks in the neighborhood, identifying places that Hazel might have taken shelter. It bothers Anne that they didn't fill in the details of Hazel's death, or how she fell from the tiny, four-paned window. Had she jumped? Would her ghost sustain the injuries that Hazel's body had incurred? Would she limp forever, with scrapes that never healed? Anne had also obsessed over Kayla, imagining tearful apologies and long kisses. She vacillated between assuring herself that Kayla wouldn't have kissed her if she didn't love her, and admonishing herself for thinking that Kayla would have any real sustained interest in her. Anne played out absurd scenarios that would delay her family's move. What if her father was fired from his company before they could transfer him? What if there was a horrible epidemic that spread through Ohio and no one was allowed to enter the state?

When Kayla arrives they go immediately up to the attic. They have no excuse to be up there; the attic is almost entirely bare now. Everything has been packed and brought downstairs. A few paint cans sit in the corner next to a bit-less drill. Dirt and hair have been swept up into little piles. Anne imagines discovering tiny footprints in the dust.

Kayla lies down on her back, fanning her hair out behind her, as if nothing has changed between them. Anne lies down next to her, pivoted, so they form two sides of a triangle.

"I'm sorry I told them about your adoption. I know you like to keep these things private. I really like you."

"Why?" Anne asks. "Why do you like me?"

"Not for the reasons you probably suspect."

"Okay. Then why."

"Because there's a lot to you, things people can't see right away. You aren't like my other friends. And you draw so well." Kayla laughs. "And you're pretty, but you don't know it."

Anne takes Kayla's hand. Kayla's nails are painted a dark shade of purple. Anne tries not to think of another girl applying the paint, of someone else holding Kayla's long, thin fingers.

"Why do you like me?" Kayla asks Anne.

"How could I not? You're perfect."

Kayla's laugh is deep and low from lying on her back. "I'm boring. I'm just like everyone else."

Anne jerks up onto her elbow and stares wide-eyed at Kayla, which makes Kayla blush. "You can't really believe that," Anne says. She lies back down and thinks. "You do whatever you want, and you're not afraid of anything. You're smart. Everything you do, you do easily."

The girls put their open palms together, as if they are high-fiving, but they hold them there, studying them. They sit up and begin to kiss. Anne stops thinking about everything except the places where their bodies come into contact.

When Kayla curves her palm around Anne's breast, pulling on the fabric of Anne's shirt, Anne doesn't know how to react. Kayla puts her lips against Anne's neck, and then runs her tongue behind Anne's ear. She moves her thumb against Anne's nipple and Anne's whole body flashes hot.

Anne knows this is the kind of thing that happens, of course. But it never seemed related to her love for Kayla. All Anne's daydreams only made it as far as kisses and handholding, or Kayla's arm draped possessively over her shoulder at a high school dance. Anne's a girl whose back-up plans have back-up plans. She can't believe that she never decided what she would do in this situation. Kayla slides her hand under Anne's shirt, and Anne pulls away.

"What do you think you're doing?" Anne demands. It's a line ripped from television dramas. A line girls hurl at overeager boys who use phrases like 'going all the way' with their terrible jock friends.

"I thought you were attracted to me," Kayla says.

Anne thinks about this assertion for what is probably a beat too long. "I am."

"You're not sure," Kayla says. "You don't know if you like girls."

Anne shakes her head. She doesn't understand what other girls have to do with the way she feels about Kayla.

"Are you worried about what people will think?" Kayla asks. "You don't have to tell anyone."

"No. I want to be with you. Just not like that."

"Then like what? I thought you *liked* me," Kayla says, and there is anger in her voice.

"I do. I like kissing you. I want..." Anne's too ashamed to continue. "Not right now."

"You're leaving in *two days*."

"Where did you even learn to do things like that?"

"Where do you think?" Kayla's cheeks flush and her eyes narrow.

"No, never mind. I don't care. I love you," Anne offers. "I'm in love with you."

"Anne."

"It's true. When I move, we can stay together. We can talk on the phone."

"Together?" Kayla threads her fingers through Anne's. "I like you so much," she says. "I really do. But you're moving."

"I'll find a way to stay here. Somehow." She can sense Kayla pulling further away from her. "When I'm with you, I don't feel afraid of anything. And I'm afraid of *everything*."

"I'm sorry."

Anne begins to cry. "I was all alone before you. And I'm going to be all alone again."

"You won't be," Kayla says, patting Anne's hand. "We can talk on the phone, like you said."

"I could stay with your family," Anne says. "I could stay with you at your house for the year."

Kayla laughs and her eyes drift to the door. "You know that wouldn't work. Right?"

Anne is having trouble breathing. Kayla holds Anne until her crying slows and then gives some excuse about needing to leave to visit her grandmother.

Anne follows Kayla downstairs. As Kayla steps outside, Anne stops her. "We never figured out how Hazel died," she says.

"We made her up," Kayla says, her eyebrows furrowed. They hug goodbye, and then the screen door is slamming shut and then Anne's whole chest is on fire and then Anne tries to allow air into her lungs like her mother taught her to and then she hears a ringing in her ears.

*

Anne doesn't remember how she gets to her room, but here she is. She cries big heaving sobs that are so consuming they shut out all her other thoughts, which is at least a small relief. Her mother knocks on her door. When Anne shouts at her to go away, her mother enters anyway. She sits on the edge of the bed and takes Anne in her steady arms.

"Anne," her mother says over and over. "It's okay." She rocks her. "I promise you, you'll make new friends."

"I won't."

"It seems that way now. But people can adjust to anything. You haven't been through it yet, but you'll see. Even when things seem impossible, even when the worst happens, you just get through it."

"What if you don't?"

"You do."

"What if *I* don't? What if *I* can't? I can't do anything normally. I can't do anything right."

"You do so much right," her mother says. "You're so good at so many things."

"You don't understand," Anne says. "I can't leave. I couldn't take it." If she only had more time, she'd be able to win Kayla back.

Her mother pulls away so she can look Anne squarely in the face. "Help me understand."

Anne shakes her head, her thick hair falling over her eyes.

"Listen to me." Her mother brushes the hair aside, and lifts Anne's chin until Anne meets her stare. "I know it doesn't seem like it's possible now, but you'll fall in love again. You'll love other people."

A shockwave runs through Anne's body. Maybe she misheard her mother. How could her mother, who is always saying stupid things like 'you're a tough nut to crack,' have such knowledge of her most private thoughts?

Her mother smiles at her, a big, goofy grin that Anne is supposed to accept as a peace offering. "It's okay. I remember what it was like. The first time always feels as if it'll be forever, as if you'll never love again. But you will."

Anne won't. Anne won't *ever* love again. She thinks of everything that had to line up perfectly to get to those few hidden kisses in the attic: the unlikely coincidence of their friendship, the spell of the attic and the thrill of the ghost story, the quirks of their personalities that complement each other just right, and the puzzle of their lips fitting together. And why would she ever want to love again, even if she could? Why would she welcome the overwhelming weight of it or the frantic, trapped thing trying to escape from inside of her? Maybe love is certain and inevitable for other people, but it's not for Anne.

"What are you thinking?" her mother says. "Really. I'm not upset about you two. And with a girl—I don't care about that." She laughs. "Actually, I almost prefer it."

Maybe the world would be better if no one spoke to each other. All the things that Anne might say to her mother—the angry things and the grateful things and the hurtful ones—melt together in her mouth. The words form a dense hot lump at the back of her throat. The burning is familiar, almost like a memory. Or like someone else's memory. Like a memory that someone once told her about.

"Please say something."

There is a long pause—a longer pause. "Anne," her mother says, sharply. "*Say* something."

"I won't," Anne manages.

They sit there, waiting for the other to move. Her mother loosens her grip. "Why are you afraid to let me know what you're feeling?"

Anne's throat is so hot that it's painful. She imagines opening her mouth so that flames can shoot out and swallow the room, singe the curtains, lick the ceiling black.

"Let it out," her mother says. "Tell me what you're thinking. Please."

"Like you told Dad that you don't want to move to Ohio? Or like you told me about your miscarriages? That you finally had to settle for me after your *third* try."

Her mother lets go of her and leans back.

"I should be allowed to have secrets, too," Anne says.

"You're nothing *but* secrets. Sometimes it's like I don't even know who you are."

Anne likes the sound of that. She gets off her bed and walks quickly to the attic stairwell. She pulls the door shut behind her and flicks the lock into place. She climbs the stairs and picks up a half-empty paint can. She opens the top and dumps the paint onto the floor. The white splotch against the dark floorboards is like a reverse hole; it looks like the floor is the empty space and the paint spill is the only thing solid. Anne swings the canister against the window as hard as she can. Her mother shouts her name at the sound of breaking glass.

Anne lies down flat on her back on the bare floor. Her body feels light, like a clean, porous object. It's her spirit that weighs her down. She squeezes her eyes shut and tries to pretend she's only a body. Her mother continues to call to her and rattle the doorknob. There's an awful thwacking sound as the flesh of her mother's palm strikes the attic door. Outside, a blue jay shrieks and shrieks and shrieks. Anne plugs her ears tightly, but even then she can't find silence. She hears the steady thumping of her pulse: her little heart, digging, digging.

The Nightmares of Jennifer Aiken, Age 29

I. Judgment

You duck into a church doorway to get out of the rain. You should have accepted Kora's offer of a ride home, but you'd thought the storm would hold off until the afternoon. Besides, you didn't want to seem needy. You and Kora have only been seeing each other for a few weeks, and you're someone who can always find your own way home. Your hair sticks in dark clumps to your neck and chest and your feet slosh in your shoes. A gust of wind blows a sheet of rain into the archway and you try the church door. It swings open and you stumble inside. When the door clicks shut, the noise from the storm fades to a low hum. Since you're still wearing last night's low-cut dress, you're glad that you haven't walked in on a service. There doesn't seem to be anyone else inside. You take off your wet heels and go sit in one of the pews.

You haven't been to a church service since you graduated from high school, over a decade ago. Even when you visit your parents, who are regular churchgoers, you sleep late on Sundays. Your mother has finally stopped nagging you about this. She finds plenty to nag you about anyway: how little you call her, who you choose to date, the state of your apartment, the second glass of wine you have at dinner, the clothes you wear.

You ring out your soaking hair and wind it into a long a coil. The church is cool and damp, like a basement. Above the altar, the statue of Christ is especially gruesome. His expression seems to reflect malice instead of divinity. You wonder what denomination the church is and consider praying, since you're here. But the thought of praying after all these years makes you laugh out loud. The noise echoes off the angles of the vaulted ceiling and comes back to you as the sound of a child giggling. You shiver. Churches have always given you the creeps.

Abruptly you rise and take three long strides towards the door, but you're halted by a man's urgent whispering. When you stop moving the noise stops with you. You scan the dark room and feel the blood pulsing in your head. Then, distinctly, you hear the voice rasping again, above you. You glance up at the choir balcony and see the silhouette of a branch scratching against one of the stained glass windows. You let out your held breath.

You start towards the door again but realize you've forgotten to grab your shoes. You run back to the pews and drop to your knees to search under the seats. Out of the corner of your eye you see a woman materialize in the shadows. You jerk up and crack the back of your head against the bottom of the bench. A high-pitched buzz fills your skull and your vision blurs. When the pain subsides enough, you scramble to your feet and discover that you've freaked yourself out over a statue of the Virgin Mary.

"You're not so scary," you say to the statue. "But fuck my shoes. I'm getting the hell out of here." When you reconsider what you've said and where you've said it, you whisper, "I'm so sorry." Then you feel impossibly silly—apologizing to a statue. A gust of wind throws rain against the windows. Wet leaves slap dully against the glass. But when the wind dies, a softer, closer rustling remains. Then: a noise like a person cooing to a newborn.

"Hello?" you call. The rustling continues, and through the balcony balustrade you see something white moving. "Who's up there?" A low pained call escapes from behind the railing. You turn and sprint for the exit but slip in a spot of wetness, scraping your knee hard. You try to get up too quickly and your ankle gives out. You crawl forward on your hands and knees, but you can't help looking behind you. You watch, a cold panic spreading through your body, as a white figure writhes and flops against the railing and then slips through an opening in the bars. You see wings flapping and hear a horrible high screech as a small squat creature half-flies, half-falls to the floor. You scream, and your scream cuts through the quiet like a freight train, extending long after you've closed your mouth. The demon, writhing on the floor, resembles a hunched bird.

It is a bird. A large white owl with one wing unnaturally bent hobbles near the organist's bench. You climb carefully to your feet and test your ankle, which is tender but not sprained. "It's okay, little guy," you say, approaching it. "Poor baby. How'd you get in here?"

The owl leans back and fixes its black eyes on your face.

"Stay away from me, you whore," the owl says, and then it lifts its head and lets loose a laugh that sounds like metal being ground to dust.

II. Proximity

When you notice movement outside the sliding glass doors of your first-floor apartment, you mute the television. You watch the dark yard for a full minute but you don't see anything unusual. Whatever was moving is still. This is what happens when you stay home alone on a Friday night. Your mind starts to play tricks on you. When you consider how nice it would be to have someone to curl up next to on the couch, you almost regret breaking it off with Kora for what you've decided will definitely be the final time. She was starting to feel like your shadow instead of your girlfriend. In your last fight, she'd tearfully informed you that you'd eventually leave her because all bisexual women leave their girlfriends for men. At least you haven't proved her right. You didn't leave her for anyone else; you left her because she was desperate and a little pathetic, and everyone deserves better than pathetic. Although, the fact remains that you're home alone on a Friday night watching *Gilmore Girls* in your pajamas. So maybe you're a little pathetic yourself. You check your phone. Chrissie, who should know you might need a little cheering up on a night like this, hasn't texted you back.

A few minutes later you see something moving by the bushes again and this time it's unmistakable. Something is pacing back and forth in the yard, and that something moves a whole lot like a person. You slowly pull out your phone and get as far as dialing 9-1-1. But what would you tell the police if you called? There's something that you can't quite see moving outside your apartment complex? On screen, someone shouts and you drop your phone. You turn the volume down and tiptoe to the door. You check the lock, which is firmly in place, and then shield your eyes and put your forehead against the glass. You don't see anyone, but the hedges are overgrown and the sky is moonless. There are plenty of places to hide. When you walk back to the couch you keep your eyes pinned to the window. You consider closing the blinds but somehow that seems worse. You can't stand the idea of someone lurking out there, unseen.

You try to focus on the show. You consider calling Kora. But you don't want her in your life, you just want her on your couch for one night, and you know that isn't fair. She'd be over in ten minutes with one word from you, though, and it's tempting.

You glance back at the window and scream. A person, or a dark figure that looks like a person, is marching straight towards the door. As the figure draws closer, you see that they're holding a knife. 'It's locked, it's locked, it's locked,' you think over and over as you fumble with your phone. You force yourself to jump off the couch and flip the lamp on. The light makes the person's features sharpen, and you can see the deep holes beneath their eyes, the muscles in their jaw tightening. Even in your panic, you know this isn't right. The light shouldn't illuminate these features.

You see your own face—your mussed hair and your wide eyes—reflected as crisply and as clearly as your attacker's. You spin around just in time to see Kora raise the knife to your neck.

III. Perfection

You're walking down a suburban street that you don't recognize and your eyes won't adjust to the brightness of the day. The expansive lawns on either side of you are well trimmed and Easter green. The houses' large bay windows reflect the sunlight and when you try to peer in through the glass you have to squint and look away from the glare. Every now and then you catch a flicker of movement behind the windowpanes, but nothing outside is moving, except for you. You're not sure what you're heading towards but you know you have to keep walking. Ahead, the road ends in a cul-de-sac and a huge brick house looms at the end of the street.

As you draw nearer to the house you notice one rough patch in the otherwise immaculate lawn. The weeds don't belong here, in this flawless, sunlit place. They've gone unnoticed by the residents of the house, but you've spotted them. You realize now that this unkempt patch of grass is the reason that you've come. This is what you've been walking towards all along. You feel a kinship with this impeccable property. It is not so different from the house that you used to imagine you'd one day live in, with a family of your own. You step onto the lawn. You wind the long, fine plant tendrils around your hand until you have a hard grip on them. You pull.

At first nothing happens, except that the blades of grass dig into your balled-up fist and your muscles flex and strain. You yank again. Nothing. You clench your jaw, take several deep breaths, and then tug as hard as you can. This time you can sense the dirt shifting and the earth turning soft under the strange weeds. Something gives, and a large irregular sphere, like an oversized turnip, emerges from the ground. The shape spins, dangling from the many plant strands that are wound around your fingers. You reach out with your free hand to grab hold of it. When the sphere steadies, you can see that you're holding the small, shriveled head of a woman. The lips are frozen in a soundless scream and the eyes are wide open with clumps of dirt still stuck to the corneas. Maggots pour out of the dead woman's mouth. You try frantically to free your hand from the tangles of the corpse's green hair, but it's as if the strands are winding themselves around your fingers and tightening their grip on your wrist, as if they are the only part of the woman left alive.

IV. Ancient

For work, you have to travel to Richmond, Indiana. After your meetings you decide to explore the town, since you have the rest of the day off and it's only a two-hour drive back to Columbus. You visited Richmond once before, when you were a little girl. Your mother was visiting a childhood friend and she brought you along. Your mother's friend showed you an album of faded photographs of her and your mother as schoolgirls. Looking at your school-aged mother was like looking into a mirror. You'd cried for a full half hour at the revelation that time would one day do to you what it had done to her. Later that same day, after you'd calmed down, you visited a small park next to a rose garden. On the windowsill in your parents' kitchen, there's a Polaroid of you posing on the stone rim of a lovely fountain. The caption on the picture reads, *Jen, age 6*.

The picture is in your pocket, suddenly. You take it out and study your mother's precise, self-assured handwriting. You miss her.

At a diner in the center of town you drink burnt coffee and ask the waitress for directions to the fountain. You show her the Polaroid. The waitress's hair is blue and she has a small stud in her chin. She calls you 'ma'am.' She says she can point you to the rose garden, but she doesn't know of any fountain. An old man sitting at the counter lowers his newspaper. His skin is leathery and ill-fitting, too loose for his bones. He introduces himself as Charlie.

"I know the fountain you're talking about," he says, his voice low enough that you have to lean forward to hear him. "The foundation crumbled fifteen years ago. But the water's still running."

The waitress rolls her eyes.

"I'm not fooling around," Charlie says. "The fountain was fed from an underground spring that's still running, and it's still as clear as glass.

If you follow the walking path on the west side of the rose garden, you'll see the Madonna of the Trail statue. What's left of the fountain is a few hundred feet back from there."

You thank Charlie, pay the bill, and then you're at the rose garden. If you find the spring, maybe you'll take a picture of the remains of the fountain so you can send it to your mother. Maybe you'll take a selfie of yourself sitting on the pile of rubble, so Mom can put it next to the picture of you as a girl. *Jen, age 29.*

You find the walking path easily. The trees are just starting to lose their leaves and the air has a chilly edge to it. Soon the path becomes overgrown, and your fingers begin to sting from the cold. Just when you've decided that Old Man Charlie was only playing a trick on an out-of-towner, you spot the statue. You leave the path and the grass gets in under your pant cuffs and scratches at your ankles.

There's an old woman kneeling at the bank of the spring. When the woman hears you, she turns her face up and pulls her hands quickly back, tucking something behind her. The woman has the same leathery skin as Charlie. Her face is puckered so all her features seem to be slipping towards her nose. When she opens her mouth, a gray moth flutters out.

"I didn't mean to startle you," the old woman says. "Not many people come out here anymore."

"I'm sorry." You feel your face flush. "I'm not from here."

"How'd you find the spring?" the woman asks.

"I was here once, as a little girl. I wanted to see it again. I don't know why."

"You're still just a girl."

You laugh. "I'm not as young as I look."

The woman tries to climb to her feet, but her legs quiver beneath her. You rush to grab her arm and help her up. The woman is holding a jar full of water so clear it glistens in the sunlight.

"Is the water good to drink?"

"*Never* drink this water."

"Why not?"

The woman thinks for a moment, and you can see that she's trying to puzzle something out. "Sit with me," the woman says finally. "I'll tell you."

You sit on the one remaining ledge of the fountain, careful to leave space between her and you. Up close, you feel a guilty disgust for the woman's decrepit features and the baby powder smell her body gives off.

The woman asks you if you believe in magic. You don't, but she is peering at you so earnestly that you shrug and tell her that maybe you could be convinced. And then she launches into her tale. She explains that the water from the spring comes from deep within the earth and has special properties. Anyone who drinks from it will extend their life for decades longer than they would normally live. She says that she is well over a hundred years old. She tells you that the fountain, once celebrated, has since been destroyed and forgotten by most of the people in town.

"An actual fountain of youth?" you ask to humor her.

"Not youth, no. More like longevity. That's why it was destroyed. Because once you drink from it, you grow old too quickly. And then you stay old for one hundred years. Your teeth will fall out, your hair will grow wispy and gray, and your bones will turn as brittle as ice. But you won't have the mercy of death, at least not for a long, long time." The woman shakes her head. "It's no way to live. It's cruel, what time does to all of us. When everyone you love is wasting away and dying, and your own body betrays you."

"I'm sorry," you say, trying to think of an excuse to leave. "That must be so hard."

"But I've sealed my fate. I have to keep drinking it to at least keep some strength up. But you must not *dare* drink. Promise me."

You promise her. "But I'm late now. I have to go. I have to get back."

"Of course you do. Because when you're young you have people waiting for you. When you're young, time matters. You have things that fill your day. That's good. Be glad for that now."

"It was nice meeting you," you say. "I hope things get better. I'm sure they will."

"Yes. I'm out of sorts today, but you're right. Things aren't so bad." The woman's voice breaks. She's close to crying.

"Goodbye. I'm sorry I can't stay." Your underarms are sweating. You stride quickly towards the path, and when you look back you see the old woman drinking hungrily from the jar, her throat expanding and contracting with each swallow. The woman drinks until there is no more water, and then raises a boney hand to wave goodbye.

On the way back to town, you jump at every small crackling in the trees. You quicken your step and check behind you. You half expect that any minute the woman will appear, sprinting with unnatural speed, clawing at you with her skeletal hands. Was she delusional or just recounting a local myth? Perhaps she was purposefully messing with you. Or she just wanted someone to talk to. A lonely, sad woman reached out to you, and you fled as soon as you could. You try to reassure yourself that she must have children and grandchildren waiting for her. She'll bring them freshly squeezed lemonade that she made with the cold spring water and they'll laugh over how Grandma spooked a city girl.

When you arrive at the rose garden, you find someone tending to the flowers. You're so relieved to find a person who looks like she's from this world that you say hello. You remark on how strange it is that the flowers still grow in October.

"Rumor has it that there's something magical in the groundwater in this part of town," the woman says.

She seems so warm and young and friendly. You want to shake off the encounter with the old woman, and you think perhaps talking about it will help. You tell her all about your experience at the fountain.

"That's quite a story she told you. She's just messing with you, I'm sure."

"Of course I don't believe any of it. But to see the way the woman drank that water down, in three big gulps, it made me queasy."

The woman's face clouds over. She drops the spade she's been using. "She drank from it? You're sure?"

"Yes," you say, backing towards your car. You wonder if everyone in this small town is a little unhinged. "So what?"

"We have to get back there. I have to call someone." The woman yanks off her gardening gloves.

You waver, fighting the impulse to flee. "I don't understand."

"That spring is toxic. It's full of arsenic."

Your head begins to throb. You close your eyes and see the old woman drinking hungrily. You see her watery eyes watching you walk away. You see the small, wilted hand raised in one last salute.

V. Reason

It starts with the sound of footsteps pacing outside the bedroom door in your new apartment, even though you live alone. You're spending the night there for the first time. When you get the nerve to jump out of bed and throw open the door, there's nothing in the hall. About half an hour later, the footsteps start again. And then there's giggling.

You turn on the light, grab your phone, and walk into the hallway. You creep into the kitchen. In the middle of the tile floor is a ratty teddy bear. When you stoop to pick up the toy, it disintegrates and seeps through your fingers like sand.

You're a reasonable person. You believe in evolution and science and logic. You mostly do not believe in ghosts. But how else can you explain this? You think of calling Chrissie or your mother, but you know you'll sound ridiculous. You're just overtired and spooked from the unfamiliar apartment, and the teddy bear was just a trick that your mind is playing on you. You're not in danger. Ghosts probably don't exist. The apartment isn't haunted.

You open the cupboard and pull out a glass. Before you can fill it with water, you notice a small ivory-colored bead on the bottom of it. You tip the glass over and catch the stone, and find that it's a small tooth. It looks like a baby tooth that someone might leave for the tooth fairy. You throw it into the sink and wipe your palm on your shirt. You take a step back and feel a sharp pain in your heel. When you lift your leg up, you find another tooth lying on the floor. You rush into your bedroom. You pull back the covers and discover three more teeth contrasted starkly against the navy blue sheets.

On the far side of your bedroom, a shadow morphs into a human form. When you examine it more closely, the shadow expands and bleeds into an amorphous splotch, blending in with the patterns of light that your lamp throws against the wall. You hear giggling—a little girl's giggling—coming from the closet, and you know you have to get out of the apartment.

You grab your purse and race outside in your bare feet. You pull out of the parking lot so fast that the undercarriage of your car scrapes the curb ramp. You don't believe in ghosts because you're rational, but a rational person considers new evidence. And there is a lot of evidence supporting the idea that your new apartment is pretty fucking haunted. You call Chrissie when you're already halfway to her place.

Sitting on Chrissie's couch with a cup of tea in your hands, you can't stop shaking. You want Chrissie to take you seriously. You're trying to seem calm. You're going to need to find a new apartment. In the meantime, you might have to stay with Chrissie and her husband for a while. You explain about the footsteps, the teddy bear, and the teeth. You start shaking when you talk about the shadows and the giggling. Chrissie gives you the look that she usually reserves for when you talk about dating—about the new girlfriend who will be perfect, as soon as she stops talking quite so much about her ex.

"Sweetie," Chrissie says, putting a warm hand on your knee. "It sounds like you're driving yourself crazy. You've totally spooked yourself. It's all in your mind."

"You didn't hear the noises. You didn't see that shadow. They were real."

"You've been so stressed lately. Moving is tough. I know you haven't been sleeping. You need to relax."

"What about the teeth? How do you explain the teeth?"

"I don't know. They're probably just pebbles or something. What did you do with them?"

"What do you think I did with them? I threw them out!"

"Listen, Jen. You're welcome to stay here until you calm down, but this is all in your mind, okay?"

You notice something stirring in the corner of Chrissie's living room. You look past Chrissie and see the blurry figure of a small girl. The girl smiles, and her mouth is a cave of pink. She has no teeth. You pull backwards and spill your tea, which causes a quick stab of pain on your stomach. Chrissie looks behind her to see what you've reacted to.

"What? What's happening?" Her voice is filled with concern.

"You don't..." You stop. Chrissie doesn't see the girl. Chrissie wouldn't hear the footsteps. No one else would see the teeth. "It's nothing," you say. "I think you're right. I think it's all in my mind."

VI. Doubt

You start awake in your own dark bedroom. You can't quite remember the nightmare you were just having, but the imprint of its terror still flashes with every beat of your heart. At first, you're afraid to move and afraid to examine the shadowy expanse of your room. But after several tense moments the fear begins to become muted. You still taste the sourness of adrenaline on the back of your tongue, but you also feel a rush of relief. Whatever threat was looming over you in sleep is gone. You're facing the wall, and you roll over to take in your bedroom. All is as it should be. Your desk sits unassumingly, cluttered with assorted objects that you've unpacked but haven't yet found a place for. Your jeans are draped across a chair. The clock reads 5:47. It's almost daybreak. You can lay back and wait for the light.

Although you're sure nothing's wrong, your muscles still pulse with tension and you can't bring yourself to close your eyes. You listen to a low steady humming—white noise from the refrigerator or the telephone wires outside. You're still adjusting to the sounds of the new apartment. You pull the blanket tighter around you, even though you're sweating.

You wipe the sweat away from your temples, and then reach for the wetness at the nape of your neck. What you touch is not the thin consistency of sweat. It is thick and viscous, like saliva or slime. You jerk your hand away, and examine the strange gelatinous liquid. When you pull your fingers apart the slime clings to itself and stretches, the way drool would. You frantically search the dark corners of your room, but, as far as you can see, you are alone.

Warnings

We'd been warned about running alone. We'd also been warned about walking at night, about bus stops and Uber drivers, about the hungry shadows of parking garages. We'd been warned and we'd warned one another about parties at Joe DiCarlos's house, Sarah's older brother, the lacrosse players who sat at the lunch table closest to the pizza station.

We heeded most of the warnings most of the time. But we were runners. And no one told the boys team to practice in pairs or avoid wearing headphones at night. Besides, when we ran, who could touch us? When we ran, in the peach light of an early sunset or in the long gray dawn, we were of the world but not in it.

So that fall afternoon when Lucy darted ahead of us, we only thought: *Showoff.* It was just practice during a week without a meet. There was no need to leave the pack so soon. Lucy was fast, probably the fastest among us, but she didn't always win her races. She couldn't pace herself. She was usually so quiet and controlled, but sometimes at the start of a race she vibrated with a fierce energy that she couldn't rein in.

We figured we'd pass her in a mile, easy, our legs chipping away steadily as she flagged. But after a mile and a half we still hadn't caught her. We leaned a little further into the wind, lifted our legs higher.

At mile two, no one even joked about stopping at Dunkin' Donuts when our course swung us by its orange lettering. We concentrated on our form. We measured our breathing. The metal taste that came to us during meets appeared. We wanted to beat her.

She was our teammate, yes, but she always held herself a little apart. She did pre-calc problem sets on the bus to meets, declined rides home after practice, and never shared secrets at team sleepovers. She was Coach Walton's favorite.

At mile three, Maria Elena finally said, "Where *is* she?"

"She can't be far. We got this."

"No. We should have caught her already."

"Maybe she veered off for a quick study break," Rylan said.

"Do you think she's okay?" Maria Elena asked. "It's weird."

What options did we have? We kept running. We thought she'd be there at the end, waiting for us. A quick glance at her watch to hint at her disappointment.

We finished the run, did our cool down exercises, joked about our numb noses, and—still—there was no sign of her. Coach Walton asked where Lucy was. We wondered if he'd notice so quickly if any of *us* were absent. We shrugged. She was with us and then she wasn't.

And then she wasn't. And then she wasn't. And then she still wasn't.

We backtracked. We texted. We called her name. We checked the Dunkin' Donuts. We paired off and fanned out. We tried to remember: who were her close friends? Later, there were police dogs. There were flyers on every telephone pole and there was her strangely stoic mother on the Channel 4 News. And later, much later, there was her body by the bank of a river on the other side of town, her team t-shirt tangled in the branches of a nearby bush.

In interviews, we told the police, "But she was *running*."

How could we explain? How could we make them see? When we ran, we removed ourselves from the world and all the traps it'd set for us. When we ran, our bodies were only ours. When we ran, we were out of reach.

"Nothing bad could've happened," we insisted in those first interviews. "She was so fast."

Here in the Night

Ellie and Jess are driving down Highway 17, away from South Carolina's Winyah Bay. They're coming from a visit with Ellie's parents, headed to the airport and then back to Maine, where they've lived together for five years. The first several miles were lit with motel signs and seafood shacks and passing cars, but now it's so dark, the only things visible outside the cone of the rental car's headlights are a thumbnail moon and a spray of stars. They've driven past the café where Ellie used to sling fried clams to sunburned tourists, the field in which Hurricane Hugo had stranded two shrimp boats, and Ellie's grandmother's little yellow cottage with its gingerbread trim. Ellie has pointed out these landmarks to Jess on previous drives, but tonight the car is quiet.

It's June 12, 2016. Some of you already know what this means. It means that in the early hours of the morning a man walked into a gay nightclub in Orlando, Florida and opened fire, killing forty-nine people in a place that was supposed to be their haven. It means fifty-three wounded. It means Ellie crying in bed that morning as she scrolled through Twitter. It means Jess wondering why she hasn't cried yet. It means Ellie's mother trying to console them, even though she still stage whispers the word 'lesbian' every time she says it. It means Jess telling Ellie to stop checking her phone if it only makes her sadder. It means Ellie accusing Jess of being strangely unmoved by the tragedy. It means guilt at being safe and alive and able to bicker, able to make up. It means that by the time they're on their way to the airport, exhaustion has settled thickly around them.

Static cuts into the song on the radio and Ellie changes the station a few times before she finds what she's looking for: the updated death toll and then a summary of a survivor's account.

"Can we turn this off?" Jess asks. "I don't want to think about it right now."

"How can you think about anything else?"

Jess fiddles with the air conditioner and then turns her attention to the tiny slice of scenery that falls within the headlights' reach.

"Baby. That wasn't an accusation," Ellie says.

"I know. I just want to be home."

Ellie switches the radio off. "Me too. But it's always hard for me to leave my folks."

Jess knows she should let things be, but she can't resist saying, "Even today? Your dad was driving me crazy. He's so obsessed with the idea that the shooter *must* have been secretly gay."

"He was trying."

"He's been *trying* for a long time."

Jess always feels prickly and out of place on these annual visits. She looks out of place, too, with her half-shaved head and lopsided tumble of messy curls, the spindly pine trees tattooed down her arm, her knee-length boys' shorts and thick thighs. She grew up in Cambridge, Massachusetts with progressive parents and she hates that Ellie's family still refers to her as Ellie's *friend*. She hates how the couch is always made up for her so she has to sleep without the comfort of Ellie's long limbs. She hates that they can't hold hands or kiss in front of Ellie's dad.

When Jess looks back over, Ellie's crying. "I'm sorry," Jess says, putting her hand on the back of Ellie's neck, under the soft swoosh of Ellie's ponytail. "What's wrong, baby?"

"I'm *sad*," Ellie says. "Why are you acting like this doesn't have anything to do with us, like it's just something that happened to other people?"

"I can be sad and not cry."

Jess usually loves driving with Ellie. She likes how the car creates a little pocket world just for them. But now Ellie has let the horror of the day in. What Jess wants—all Jess wants—is for her and Ellie to be alone in the car without the crushing weight of other people's tragedy. She wants to free them from the tangle of other people's sorrow and other people's hate.

They hit a pothole—not even a very big one, Jess will think later—and the car begins to make a clunking sound. Ellie maneuvers it to the side of the road and the headlights catch a cloud of insects so dense it looks like a snow squall.

"Shit," Ellie says. "Shit. Shit. Shit."

"What was that?"

A car whizzes past them and their seats shake. "A flat tire, I think," Ellie says.

When Jess opens her door the air is so humid it feels thick. The chorus of insect noise sounds like millions of teeth chattering. Ellie comes around to Jess's side of the car and the bushes erupt into movement as something darts off into the high grass.

Ellie kneels by the traitorous tire and thumps the wheel well. When she gets up pebbles cling to her bare knees. A mosquito lands in the crook of her elbow. She slaps it.

"We'll miss our flight," Jess says. She's embarrassed that neither of them knows how to change a tire. But if she were to attempt any heroics, it wouldn't be on this dark road with this unfamiliar car. "What happens if we miss our flight?"

"There are other flights," Ellie says. She's already dialing AAA, putting the phone to her ear. Ellie's always the emotional one until there's a task to complete. Then she's all business. "If we need to stay another day, we'll stay another day. No big deal."

Now Jess does feel like crying, which she would never admit. She goes to the trunk to search for a long-sleeved shirt. Even in the heat, it'll be better than letting the gnats bump against her bare skin. She sits on the edge of the open trunk to wait. A little ways down the road there's a water tower perched on bowed legs. Against the velvet sky it looks like a hovering UFO.

"They'll be here in forty minutes," Ellie says. "Maybe less."

"Thanks, El."

"We probably will have to reschedule the flight," Ellie concedes. "So we might be stuck here another day. Your worst nightmare." She perches next to Jess, leaving a thin gap between their bodies that Jess longs to close.

"I *am* sad about what happened," Jess says. "But I also feel… I don't know. I can't explain it."

"Can you at least try?" Ellie can never abide a mystery. And now that Jess has had some time to think, she does want to explain.

"I don't know if you remember this," Jess says. "But last year there was a story in the *Times* about a funeral home in Mississippi that wouldn't pick up the body of an eighty-year-old man after they found out he was gay."

"I remember," Ellie says.

"I read the article while I was eating breakfast. It upset me so much that I had to throw away the rest of my toast. But I didn't cry then, either. I felt angry, or like I should be angry. Mostly I wished I hadn't read it. It felt so awful to be reminded, before I'd finished my coffee, that there are people in this country who wouldn't even lay my body to rest."

"I don't need a newspaper to remind me of that," Ellie says. She takes Jess's hand. It's the first time she's held it since they got off the plane a week ago.

"But that's not our lives. At least not in Portland."

"Enough of that," Ellie says, swatting the air. "Maine is not better than here."

"But *isn't* it?" Jess says, laughing. Then she adds, "I'm sorry I make these trips difficult. I'm a true New Englander. We're wary of everything."

"Especially outsiders," Ellie says. "Like me."

"Not to be trusted," Jess agrees.

She leans in and kisses Ellie. The kiss is slow and deep and reminds Jess of kisses from early in their relationship, before things between them became so steady and certain.

They're still kissing when a green pick-up truck rumbles into view. The sound of the horn makes them jerk apart. There are two men in the cab. The driver is leaning over the passenger to shout at them through the open window. They don't understand the first part of what he yells, but the sentence ends with "dykes" and then an ugly bark of laughter.

As the truck passes, they take in the confederate flag decal covering the whole back window and the man in the passenger seat craning his neck to watch their reaction. They're too surprised to show any emotion, which they're grateful for. They both know that in situations like this, it's best not to react.

When the truck disappears around a bend, Jess rolls her eyes. "Assholes."

"Do you think we should get in the car and lock the doors?" Ellie asks.

"Oh, sweetie. We're okay." Jess puts her arm around Ellie and kisses her temple. Ellie stands up and steps back. "They're gone," Jess says. Ellie nods, but stays where she is. Jess furrows her brow but doesn't reach for Ellie again.

"I love you," Jess says.

"I love you, too," Ellie says softly, pulling at the frayed bottom of her shorts.

Jess swivels so she can search through the outer pocket of her suitcase, finally pulling out a deck of cards. She's about to ask Ellie to come play rummy, but Ellie is staring at the road behind Jess.

When Jess turns, she sees a pick-up drawing nearer. Against the glare of headlights she can't tell if it's the same truck, circling back. She watches the orange glow of the blinker as the truck eases to the side of the road. She listens to the pop of gravel under the tire treads. When the truck comes to a full stop, there's no doubt that it's the same one. Jess stands and joins Ellie. They link arms.

The driver looks middle-aged. One side of his jaw droops slightly. "It seems like you ladies are stranded," he calls across the empty road. There's something in his voice—a forced and teasing lightness—that would set off Jess's alarm bells even if she weren't already on edge.

Jess tries to think of the magic words that will keep the men inside their truck, away from her and Ellie. Nothing comes. She can only shake her head.

"I'm happy to help," the driver says.

"Thank you, but we've got things under control," Jess says.

"It sure doesn't seem like it." The man laughs.

Ellie is scanning the brush behind them, perhaps considering escape routes. Jess wonders if their fear is an overreaction, fueled by the stress of the day and the night's inky blackness and the isolation of the rural road. She wonders what they'll do if the worst happens. She wonders if next week someone will read an article about this and be unable to finish her toast.

The driver opens his door and steps out onto the road.

*

And, I'll tell you: they survive this. They survive, shaken but unharmed. They survive and they get back to their small third-floor apartment that catches the sunlight and glows like amber for half an hour every day. They get back to their six-toed orange tabby. To the waft of hot ginger-scented air that escapes the bathroom when Ellie gets out of the shower. To Jess rubbing her feet together like a praying mantis to get off any dirt before she climbs into their shared bed. To their bed. To books with cracked spines, to grumbles about alarms going off too early, to an extra ten minutes of stolen sleep. To their heavy door that keeps the noise out. To their quiet, complex lives, which are, on the whole, happier and calmer than either of them expected.

You can know this, but they cannot. And so, in this long and jagged moment, the sound of the truck door opening is like a gunshot. Even the bugs seem to quiet; even the wind seems to stop. And their hearts are rioting in the cages of their chests, and their limbs are pulsing, and their bodies are electric, and they are ready to flee, together, into the hot and waiting night.

The Elevator Girl

I didn't know I'd become a campus legend until the reporter from *The Lantern* called. I was still living in Ohio, about an hour northeast of Columbus, but I hadn't been back to OSU in over twenty years. I was impressed that AJ had found me. All she had was my first name, Grace, and the story about my awful night in the elevator. She didn't even know my class year, so she'd spent weeks emailing inquiries to art department alumni. She was writing a follow-up to a Halloween fluff piece called "Haunted Ohio State: The Ghosts of Buckeye Past."

At first I made excuses about not wanting to dredge up difficult memories, but I was charmed by how seriously she took her student job and the boldness of cold-calling me instead of emailing. And it was the day after New Year's. AJ should've been home on break, like my wife's daughter, who was sleeping until eleven every day and leaving Diet Coke cans all over the house. I remembered the eerie stillness of the dorms during the holidays and felt a sense of kinship with AJ.

"All right," I said as I settled into the couch. "Let's start with what you already know."

*

The Grace from the legend that AJ recounted was a strange and obsessive student. She kept weird hours and often worked through the night in her studio, painting huge canvases that she only ever showed her favorite professors. One of these late nights, she got stuck in the elevator after the building had emptied out. As the hours stretched on, she lost her grip on reality. She beat the doors until her hands were bruised and bloody and then drew cryptic symbols all over the walls. When the custodian discovered her the next morning, she talked only in grunts. She died a few years later under vague but mysterious circumstances. Her furious ghost returned to the art building to get revenge on the university and all the happy, still-sane students. She stopped the elevator between floors, scrawled angry messages on the walls, plunged the elevator into darkness, hummed a disquieting, wordless tune, and watched with disdain as undergrads cowered in the corner and jabbed at the door open button.

"So obviously you're not dead," AJ said, "which has really broken this story wide open. But aside from that small detail, how much of the story is accurate?"

"I could speak when I was rescued," I said. "Though I probably wasn't making much sense. Other than that, it's pretty close."

"Can we meet?" she asked.

I figured I might as well finish what I'd started, so I told her the name of the coffee shop in town and we made a date for the next day.

*

AJ was waiting for me at a corner table, her tea already half-empty. She was more awkward in person than she'd been on the phone. Her clothes didn't fit right and her expression always hinged towards apologetic. But I could tell she'd come into her own later, like I had—one of the lucky girls that life gets better for instead of worse.

"I don't want you to use my real name if you print anything I tell you today," I said. Then I began—I don't know why—with the full backstory. That it was Thanksgiving. That I wasn't welcome home that break because I'd just come out as a lesbian to my very Christian parents. That I hadn't been eating well. That I was very sad and very lonely. That I threw myself into my artwork because it was the only thing that made me feel good, which is why I was working late on a holiday instead of eating store-bought mashed potatoes in my dorm room.

The art building was spooky at night—high-ceilinged and drafty and filled with peculiar sculptures—so I was already on edge as I put away my paints. There were so many places someone could be hiding. I relaxed when I stepped into the elevator, but after just a few moments of shaky descent, it juddered to a halt. Then, the lights and all the mechanical sounds in the building turned off in slow motion, like the reluctant closing of an eyelid fighting sleep.

I panicked. I threw myself at the doors, pressed every button, held my finger on the alarm bell until the noise began to unnerve me, and screamed until my throat ached. The darkness was so heavy I could feel it. I squeezed myself into a corner and made myself small. Eventually, I could see the outlines of my fingers if I held my hands close to my face and some gradations in the shadows, but that was almost worse. I tried to pry the doors apart. When I had them open a few inches I saw that I was stuck. The floor above me was too high for me to climb to and directly in front of me was a concrete wall. When I looked down, there was a small gap that led into the dizzying emptiness of the elevator shaft. The lights in the building were off, but the moon and the green glow of an emergency exit sign on the floor above me gave some light. I took off my boots and stuck them between the doors, and then settled back into my corner, wide-eyed, watching the dusky space around me.

After what was probably an hour, I had calmed down enough to think. I hadn't eaten all day and I was feeling light-headed. I wondered if I should rest, so I'd be alert when morning came and there was a slight chance I would be heard. The university was closed for the long weekend, which meant it could be days before someone else entered the building. I put my head on my knees.

I never wore a watch back then, so I can't say how long it was before I started to hear scratching. I moved to the center of the elevator, because I assumed it was something outside, wanting in. The scratching continued, on and off—a horrible visceral sound, like an animal clawing at burlap.

Gradually, the elevator filled with the stink of cheap beer, throw-up, and the brand of deodorant my ex-boyfriend used to wear. One of the shadows in the elevator thickened, sharpened, and then became my ex-boyfriend, who'd been dead for a year. He was sitting with his knees pulled up to his chest and scratching at his eczema, a habit that had repulsed me even when he was still alive. Piles of skin flakes had collected at his feet, as if he'd been there for hours. Vomit stained the front of his t-shirt.

He died alone in bed on a night I'd refused to come over, drunk and choking on his own throw-up. Back then, I believed it was my fault that he was dead. Because I hadn't gone over, and also because of how badly I'd wanted him to disappear. And, after sitting through all those sermons with my parents, there was a part of me that believed his death, or maybe just my guilt over his death, was my punishment for being the way that I was.

He continued to scratch, raising jagged welts on his forearms. I was too scared even to scream. I considered forcing myself through the thin gap in the doors and jumping. But I couldn't will myself to move, and didn't dare turn my back on him.

He was looking at me with only vague recognition. He inched towards me and I inched away. We circled the elevator. When I couldn't take it anymore and let him get close enough to touch me, he slipped his meaty fingers under my sock and wrapped them around my ankle. He ran his thumb over the bone there, making tight circles. He dragged his hand up to my knee and I recoiled. "You don't get to touch me anymore," I croaked.

He cocked his head to the side and said, in a voice that was slower and thicker than his own, something that sounded like, "You're invited."

His edges rippled slightly and he turned into something that was between states of matter, something voluptuous and contemptuous and wanting. And the thing that was in him never took its eyes off me.

I waited for dawn to come and rescue me. It seemed impossible that the thing in the elevator with me could exist in the daytime. And I felt that I'd be ready to die as long as I was alone, as long as there was daylight. But when the pink smear of sunrise arrived and angles of light pierced the floor above me, the thing that was sharing my ex-boyfriend's dead flesh did not leave.

It wasn't until another art student came in that afternoon and answered my cries of distress that the smell of vomit and beer and rotten meat dissipated and I was alone again.

*

AJ toyed with her empty cup and tucked her pen behind her ear. Her notebook page was filled.

"How often do you think about that night?" she asked.

"For a while, it was every day. Now, only when I'm reminded."

"How did you survive all those hours? You must have been terrified."

"I didn't have a choice," I said. "I tried to distract myself. I hummed old songs that my mother used to sing for me. I do that, still, when I'm nervous."

"And you believe your ex-boyfriend's ghost—or something supernatural—was really in the elevator with you? You don't think it could have been a dream or... I don't know."

"It was *real*," I said.

"And do you think it's your ex-boyfriend who still haunts the elevator now?"

"I wouldn't know," I said. "But probably not. Why would he?"

"Then do you think the elevator is a special place, like a sort of window into the next world?" She seemed to regret the leading question—a lapse in her journalistic integrity—and she didn't wait for my answer. "How do you explain what happened to you?"

"I've given up trying to explain," I said. "As a rule, I don't ruminate on it anymore."

She wanted to ask more questions, but the afternoon had darkened and it had started snowing. I was worried about her icy drive back to campus. I bought her a snack for the road and made her promise to text when she got to her dorm.

After I climbed into my car, I watched AJ leave, her tires carving gray tracks in the snow. I texted my wife to let her know I was on my way home and that I was feeling mostly okay after the meeting. I massaged my temples and caught my own eyes in the rearview mirror. For a moment, I enjoyed imagining myself as the vengeful ghost from AJ's legend, righteous and angry and unforgiving. But that wasn't me. Even as a poltergeist, I'd probably be magnanimous. It hadn't ever occurred to me to fault the university, nonetheless to seek *revenge*, for that torturous night. I'd long ago forgiven my parents for turning their backs on me during those lonely years. I didn't even really blame my ex-boyfriend for all his clumsy cruelty when we were together or for whatever his ghost wanted when he came for me in that elevator.

I shivered, trying to shake off the memory, and went to put the key in the ignition. Then I felt his hand again, damp and heavy against my ankle. I reached for the tricks my therapist had taught me—counting the dials on the radio, feeling the lizard-like skin of the steering wheel beneath my palms—but I was slipping. The car filled with the smell of cheep beer and bile. I looked out the window at the flakes drifting down, and then the eyelid of the world blinked shut and opened again and I was back in that black box, in a wash of pale green light. *This isn't forever,* I thought. *This isn't forever.* My mantra for when the episodes got this far. And then the cold metal of the elevator pressed against my back. *This isn't forever.* I began to hum.

Then, through my usual panic, AJ's story returned to me. I tried to see beyond the fear. And maybe there was an extra presence, an extra warmth. I began to wonder if, at that very moment, an undergrad was rising through the shell of Hopkins Hall. I wondered if they were starting to hear quick, shallow breathing, to get the unmistakable feeling of another person's weight beside them. To smell something acrid and strange. To feel the need to tug the collar of their coat up to protect the exposed flesh of their neck. Then: the lights flickering. An odd, fleshy scratching. And a low uneven humming, as if someone was singing softly in a far-away room.

Northwood

The town of Northwood, New Hampshire, where I grew up, is known for its unusually high disappearance rate. Going back hundreds of years, the rate of missing persons cases has been alarming for such a small and otherwise sleepy town. The explanations for this phenomenon have always tended towards the mythic. It was said that there were witches in our woods, specters in our basements. The frozen ghost of a small boy lured trusting children onto the ice-covered lake. Floating yellow lights and the smell of sulfur appeared at dusk behind the Sherman's barn, where Mary Sherman had hung herself the year before I was born. Rather than shying away from these stories, we reveled in the local infamy they brought us. As a town where the population was dwindling, along with the available jobs, those of us who remained were unflaggingly loyal. We were proud of our oddities and our hauntings.

When my father disappeared the September after I turned ten, his departure felt as sudden and inexplicable as one of the rumored vanishings. My parents had been screaming at each other weekly ever since I could remember, so it didn't seem particularly unusual that the night before my father left there had been shouting through the bedroom walls. When I came home from school the next day and my father was gone, it did not occur to me that he had finally done what my mother had been threatening to do for years: he had left. But he, unlike my mother, didn't want to take me with him; he did not say goodbye. He did not go through the process of slowly extricating his life and his belongings from our lives. He packed some of his clothes and he moved out of town. It would be years before I heard from him again—years that grew thickly between us and hardened into stone.

What I knew, at ten, was only that he was gone, and his absence pressed on me in everything I did. When I woke in the mornings I listened for his heavy footsteps in the hallway or for his singing voice to rise over the rush of the shower. When I got home from school and my mother was still at work, answering phones at a doctor's office, I would kick a soccer ball against the side of our garage. I'd imagine my father coaching me, an activity the two of us had dutifully attempted together once or twice a year ever since I was old enough to kick. I had polite invented conversations with my father, telling him about the butterflies we were studying in school and the cigarette I had seen Mrs. Wallace sneaking during lunch. My father became a sort of invisible friend. In this new role he became more present in my life than he had been before he left. My father never had known quite what to make of me—a daughter so much like his wild wife. Where he was careful and stoic, we were impulsive and steered by instinct. It was a contrast that I'd always thought worked well: his restraint counterbalanced by our spontaneity.

Every night at dinner I asked my mother when Dad would be back, where he'd gone, and what had happened to him. I couldn't bring myself to ask *why* he'd gone—it was unimaginable that he would've made such a choice. My daily questions must have been torture for my mother, who didn't handle his leaving well. She would have crying fits that didn't seem to be brought on by anything at all, while she was cooking dinner, while we watched television in the evenings, as she was falling asleep at night. I overheard her on the phone, telling her best friend, Missy, that she was even getting in trouble at work, because she'd start crying right at her desk. My mother is not fragile, but her emotions run close to the surface and she isn't afraid to show them. Even still, she's sturdy and imposing; she carries herself with her shoulders back and her head up. She has eyes so dark that sometimes her pupils get lost in them, and when her stare falls on you, it often seems like a challenge or a dare.

My mother couldn't give me a clear explanation of what had happened with my father. She kept the terms of his disappearance vague, saying only that he was gone and there was a chance he wouldn't be coming back for a very long time, but not to be angry with him. Because it hurt too much to imagine my father living his life somewhere far from us, I thought of him as being in a transient realm, a place where he was neither with us nor away from us. Right from the start, I attached a certain air of mysticism to his absence.

After several weeks had passed, my mother, finally too frustrated with my questions to contain the anger that was always so close to the surface with her, slapped my face and snapped, "Listen, Lilly, you need to accept that your father is gone and he is not coming back, *ever*. As far as it concerns you and me, he has vanished off the face of this earth entirely." Her tone, and not the force of her fingers, was the real injury. I wept and told her that I hated her and I wished she'd disappeared instead of him. We had both found the quickest ways to hurt each other. The damage done, I stomped to my room and cried until my chest ached when I breathed. I tore my drawings from my walls and ripped them to shreds. I stormed until I felt empty and still. Then I slept until midnight, when my mother came to my room, nudged me awake, and hugged me before I could remember my fury.

*

That night, as I was drifting to sleep, I reconsidered the language my mother had used—the way she had said my father had *vanished from this earth*—and I began to draw some of the conclusions that had been lurking, inchoate, in my mind. Although Northwood had many tales of hauntings, the legend that was most often told was that of a beast-man with hooves for feet. I'd heard different versions of this tale whispered on the playground or told as a dramatic bedtime story by a teenage babysitter, but the basic facts always remained unchanged.

The tale explained that if you screamed at midnight, then the specter of a man with horse's hooves would appear behind you. If you had any chance of escaping him, you needed to spend the rest of the night without once turning around, all the while knowing that this monstrous shadow loomed just at the edge of your vision. If at any point you looked back upon the face of the man, he would take your soul. There was debate over what the man would do with your body. Some said he feasted on it. Some said he used victims' bones to build himself a mansion deep in the woods. Some said he kept the bodies frozen in an underground lair. Some said he took the soul and the body together, and kept them as his servants. Often, the storyteller would present all these sinister options for the listener to consider.

The beast-man lived on the edge of town, where the train tracks crossed into East Andover. Sometimes, victims would sleepwalk out of their beds to this spot, and awaken only when they heard themselves screaming into the black night. When this happened, they had to flee through the woods, back towards town, with their eyes trained only on the ground in front of them. Sometimes teenagers would walk to this spot and challenge the specter, summoning him with a scream so that they could race him home and brag about it at school the next day. But, more often than not, it was said that the temptation of glancing over their shoulders was too great. And when the ghoul caught you, no one would ever see a trace of you again, except for maybe a shoe or your dirty sweater. It would be as if you had simply vanished.

*

The next day during recess, I asked my best friend Suzanne, a girl with frizzy ringlets and wide blue eyes, if she knew the legend of the beast-man who lived on the border of town. We were sitting behind a row of evergreen bushes, our backs pressed against the cold stone of the school's foundation.

"*Everyone* knows that story, Lilly," she said. While I was often getting in trouble and spent just as much time kicking Bobby Hendricks under the table as I did listening to our teacher, Suzanne was studious and good. She was always covering for me or helping me weasel my way out of punishment, and no one ever doubted her. Despite, or maybe because of, our differences, we were inseparable. We were an *us* in a world full of *thems*. Throughout high school, and even after I went away to college, she would be there, coaching me out of scrapes, listening to me cry over heartbreaks and jealousies. And, twenty years later, I still see her every time I make the drive to visit my mother.

"Do you think he's real? The beast-man?" I asked her.

Suzanne considered this, chewing on the ends of her hair. "Yes," she said. "My cousin Jenny knew someone who went to the tracks and called him, and barely escaped through the woods. The girl heard the beat of *hooves* all the way home." Cousin Jenny was almost eighteen, and if she believed, there was no reason that we shouldn't.

"I think the beast-man took my father," I said.

Suzanne chewed on her chapped lips while she considered. "You think your dad's dead?" she asked.

"No," I said sharply. "No one knows what the beast-man does with the people he captures. He only steals the souls. Maybe he's just keeping them as prisoners."

"I've heard he does that sometimes," she said, after some thought.

"The night before Dad left, my parents were yelling as I was falling asleep. I didn't look at the time, but it must have been midnight when my father screamed."

"Have you told your mom?"

"She said I can't ask her about him anymore. She's too upset."

"I'm sorry," Suzanne said, and she took my hand. But I didn't want to be pitied.

"I'm going to ask the beast-man for my dad back," I said, pulling my shoulders back and lifting my chin up in my best imitation of my mother.

"Lilly," Suzanne hissed, her eyes growing large. She peered through the tangled branches at the rest of our class, and then dropped her voice. "You can't call the beast-man. No one our age does that."

This was the reaction I wanted. I needed a detractor to argue against to cement my conviction. "I'll do it this Saturday. I'll sneak out of the house, go through the woods to the tracks, and scream for him. But when he chases me I won't look at his face. I'll just tell him that I've come for my father. The spot by the tracks is only a few blocks from our street. If you cut through the woods you can be there in ten minutes, easy." We had wandered down to the tracks to leave pennies for the train to squash plenty of times.

"I'll go with you," Suzanne said, taking me by surprise. This show of boldness was unlike her; she was always holding back. Perhaps she knew how important this was to me, or maybe the temptation of confronting the beast-man was too much to pass up on. I had not counted on her camaraderie, and it moved me. It still moves me, thinking of how much this cautious girl must have loved me to attempt something so reckless.

*

For my mother, every Friday was girls' night. She and four of her friends, all former classmates at Northwood High, would meet up and forget about the bosses that asked them to work Sundays or cut their hours without warning, or the children who'd gotten into trouble at school again, or the husbands who left one morning and didn't come back. The women had been meeting at our place since my father left. Years later, I realized this was probably because my mother was worried about wasting money on a babysitter without my father's added income. I hated the arrangement, since I loved having babysitters to braid my hair and tell me stories and ask me questions about my life. It also meant that I had to be in bed early and stay out of the way.

That Friday, I woke at exactly midnight, just in time to watch as the clock hands joined and clicked into place. How could that not be a premonition? The beast-man was communicating with me one night early. He knew my plans. I stared into the shadows of my bedroom without breathing, waiting for some other sign. I wanted to reach over to snap on the lamp, but I was afraid of letting my bare arm extend over the side of the bed unprotected. Through my bedroom door, I could hear the muted sounds of my mother's deep laughter and the scrape of chairs in the kitchen. I rolled over and peered out the window towards the rough outline of woods, where the silhouetted treetops met the sky. Although the woods looked spooky, I felt that the spirit I was sensing was contained in my room with me. I pulled the blanket over my head like a hood and struggled to return to sleep.

My father had taught me a game for nights like this, to keep me from climbing into bed with him and my mother when I couldn't sleep. He would tell me to call to mind the image of a blue cow. From the blue cow, I was to let my mind wander freely to an equally nonsensical image—Abraham Lincoln with a beard that touched his toes, a starfish walking on two legs, a red barn that swayed with the wind. I tried the method, but I kept breaking the only rule of the game; I wasn't allowing the images to be random. Instead, I pictured the rusted stretch of railway in the dark wood, then the cloven feet of the beast-man gripping the sodden ground, then the whirlwind of leaves that I imagined must accompany the beast-man's arrival. I pictured myself, trembling but stalwart, a heroine who was not fearless, but full of fear and standing there, still. With my eyes cast down to the soil, I demanded my father back. I could be cunning, if necessary; I could crack jokes. I was sure the beast-man had a sense of humor, that he was the type of villain who would appreciate an opponent who could match his wit. When the specter finally relented, my father emerged from the trees just as the beast-man vanished. Dad looked dazed, his rust-colored hair tangled and falling over his eyes. I saw his lips peel back in a smile and noted something manufactured in the expression. For the first time, I considered what returning from the land of the dead might do to a person. What mark might it leave? What web-like tendrils did it attach to its residents and how far might these tendrils stretch before they finally snapped?

I sat up in bed and threw the covers off. I dashed from my room and down the stairs. I ran to my mother and threw my arms around her waist.

Her friends laughed and Samantha, who did not have any kids of her own, cooed, "Somebody just couldn't stay away."

"I had a nightmare," I said. "Can I stay down here with you?"

My mother exchanged a glance with Missy, and then shrugged. "Well, why not? It is girls' night after all."

"Goodie," Samantha said. "She's so sweet. Such a dream."

My mother rolled her eyes. "Oh please. She's a little she-devil," she said, but she was smiling. "Just like I was." She ran her fingers through my knotted hair.

"Was? I don't think you ever grew out of it," Missy said.

"Let's drink to that," Samantha said. The women clinked beer bottles.

"What was your nightmare about?" my mother asked after taking a long swig.

"It was about the beast-man," I said, carefully. "The one you scream for at midnight."

My mother frowned. She looked at me, but her glazed eyes didn't focus. "The beast-man. Are you kids still telling that story? The one with the man who steals your soul?" I nodded. The women murmured their approval—the vines of the legend were still growing, stretching into our consciousness, closing the gap between our generations. Northwood was still haunted, still a town full of ghosts and magic.

"That story used to terrify me," Samantha said. "Every time I was near the woods after dark, or whenever I heard the train whistle at night." She turned to my mother. Even in my mother's current vulnerable position, she was always the leader of the group. "Did you ever conjure the beast-man? That sounds like something you'd do, if any of us would."

My mother laughed. "Are you kidding? I'd never have the strength of will not to look at the beast's face." I was standing by my mother's chair, leaning against her shoulder.

"Please, Maggie. You're the most strong-willed woman I know."

"Not when it comes to things like that."

"Things like what?"

"Temptation. Self-control. Knowing what's good for me. You just take your pick. No, if I had ever called to the beast-man, I'd be a goner. Just a pile of bones in the woods."

Missy noticed that I had paled. "Maggie," she said. "You're going to give Lilly more nightmares."

"You know," Samantha said, "it's just Northwood's weird version of Lot's wife. Only we wind up with a worse fate than turning into a pillar of salt. We wind up having our souls stolen by a man with horse feet."

My mother leaned unsteadily into the table. She waved her thin fingers dismissively. "You know what I think that story's really about? That story is about falling in love." She raised her thin eyebrows. "Think about it."

"Oh, Maggie. Come on."

"Hear me out. A tall, dark, handsome man comes to you when you're at your most vulnerable."

"Who said anything about handsome?" Samantha cut in.

"When you're screaming in the middle of the night," my mother said out of the corner of her mouth.

"You're terrible," Missy said.

"And then you, like any sensible person facing something that's planning to steal your soul, try to run away. You try to resist, but when you give in—and you always give in—when you face it head on, part of you *dies*." The party grew quiet; the women shifted in their chairs and studied the pockmarked wood of our kitchen table.

"Come on, girls," my mother said. "I'm just being funny."

Missy got up and reached for my hand. "I'll bring Lilly back to bed." But I was reluctant to leave my mother's side. I gripped her knee. My mother wrapped me in her slender arms and held me too tightly. Her hair itched my face.

"But you, my little girl, aren't going to make my mistakes." She pulled me away from her. "I'll be sure of it. You're not marrying someone from your freshman homeroom. You are going to get out of this shit town and make something of yourself. You're going to have more sense than your silly mother. Promise me."

"Come on," Missy said, tugging at my hand.

"Promise me, Lilly."

"Mom," I said. "The beast-man. Did he take Daddy?"

My mother let go of me and studied my face with a puzzled expression. Then she laughed. "Something like that, sweetheart."

*

Now, at thirty, I rather like my mother's interpretation of the legend as an allegory for love. She told it in jest, but certainly it's a plausible interpretation. Love and horror are so easily conflated; the boundary between passion and terror is not always clear. And perhaps the death in my mother's version of the tale is not entirely tragic—but rather a symbolic death that one surrenders to, willingly. A death that's part of life. Why not?

After all, what is a town ghost story, if not some patchwork version of our own unique fears—a communal nightmare that ensures our children will be afraid of the same things we are? As the legend gets retold the details change to serve our varied purposes, and the interpretations differ. Now, it's clear to me where the story's origin lies. It was the fear of a dying town—a town that people were pouring out of like blood from a wound. I mean, the man snatches people and drags them to the border of town. Or worse, he compels sleepwalkers to wander there of their own accord. And his lair is near the train tracks, which once pumped life into the town, before the highways made the railroad system mostly obsolete. In some versions of the tale the beast-man is even wearing a suit, carrying a briefcase. To flee him you have to turn and race towards the town center. And you cannot look back at him, though it's tempting. This man was poaching Northwood's citizens, stealing its men and its children. He was an embodiment of that complicated small-town fear: that the success of our children necessitates abandonment of us. My mother and her friends would often gossip about the people who moved away and came home for the holidays, claiming these former residents had lost their roots. But they alternately wished for their own children to leave, to find a place that felt more relevant than the world we inhabited. My mother was desperate not to lose me, but more desperate for me to be a different kind of woman than she was, and to have an entirely different kind of life. Eventually, she would persuade me to leave Northwood for college, and then to accept a job at a biotech company in Boston, a city in which I knew no one. And heeding my mother's warning, I didn't marry Luke Harris from the ninth grade, nor did I marry any of the men I loved and cried over in college or after. But I've made the necessary connections to make a new city feel like home. I've established myself. I'm not lonely. I have what I think my mother always wanted for me: a life that no one else can easily or carelessly upheave.

My mother's interpretation that night also took on a new meaning for me years later, when my father finally contacted me. My mother, possibly fearing that my dad would reveal her secret, confessed to me that my father had actually left because he'd found out that she was sleeping with a coworker. By then I was eighteen, already less volatile than I had been as a child, and after so many years of blaming my father I couldn't revise the assigned roles of villain and ally. It didn't take me long to forgive my mother, to ease her conscience and to accept her apologies and excuses. My mother's transgression had been directed at my father; his transgression had been directed at me. And, I was old enough then to understand the difficulty of my mother's situation, the shadowy way that love and lust and desperation can blur the difference between right and wrong.

But these are things that I couldn't have comprehended at ten, when I was convinced that the beast-man had stolen my father, and that this specter had the sole power to return my life to the way it had been.

*

Saturday night I was all nerves. The immensity of what Suzanne and I were planning to do finally hit me. We were risking what we believed was the real possibility of death. But for the first time in weeks, I passed the day without a single moment of sadness. The absence of my father no longer bore on me as an emptiness. I felt full. I felt heroic and exalted. I was being tested.

At 11:30, I met Suzanne in front of her house. She lived less than a block away, but I'd run the whole way there, telling myself it was because

I was anxious to get started on our journey. Now that we'd both escaped our houses unnoticed, there was no threat of being caught. There were no cars passing by on our quiet back road. The air tasted cool and clean. We reviewed the plan once we came to the path in the woods. At midnight I would scream, and then we would run back towards town together, holding hands. We were never allowed to let go of the other person, no matter what. And then, while Suzanne kept her eyes closed, I would turn to the beast-man, but only look at his feet. And I would do all the talking. In the mirror, I had rehearsed all the things I might say to provoke the safe return of my father. We were ready.

When we stepped under the covering of trees, still clinging to their September leaves, everything darkened. Suzanne froze. "Maybe we shouldn't do this," she said. The beam from her flashlight skittered across the path, then onto the branches just above us, and then into the woods beside her. I held mine still, shining forward.

I don't remember what I said to persuade her, but there was never any real doubt that we'd continue. I was too full of want to just slink away, and Suzanne was too loyal to send me into the beast-man's territory alone. We went on. Very slowly, we picked our way through the woods. Once, I stumbled into a cobweb and shrieked, and once Suzanne fell over a log. It was strange how different the familiar woods looked at night, as if we were in a place that we had never been before. It was as exhilarating as it was terrifying. Of course these same trees had stood every night, as they stood now, whether we had seen them or not, but witnessing them in the darkness seemed like discovery. The branches overhead, silhouetted against a light that my eyes had miraculously adjusted to, swayed in an unfelt wind. I tried not to become distracted; a good explorer had to be ready and alert. Suzanne's rhythmic breathing and the warm pressure of her hand kept me focused. She trailed behind me, so close that she often stepped on the backs of my heels. Periodically, she squeezed my fingers, and I returned the gesture. There were rustlings to the sides of us, and occasionally we would stop to listen, holding the air in our lungs, afraid to blot out the noise by exhaling. We came to the tracks and stopped.

"How do we know that this is the town border?" Suzanne whispered, her eyes moving across the landscape. I hadn't thought of this. I had imagined we would instantly know when we came across the right spot. I told her that this was good enough, and that I would just have to be sure to scream loud enough for the beast-man to hear. Suzanne checked the watch that she had borrowed from her sister. It was 11:55.

We kicked at the gravel by the track and stared into the maze of trees on either side of the tracks. Not moving, waiting, we were totally unprotected. Instinctively, we stood back-to-back, posted up against unseen enemies. After a minute, Suzanne reached into her pocket and pulled out a penny. She placed it on the track.

"For later," she said, and the joke relaxed us.

At 11:58, I said, "Thank you, Suzanne."

At 11:59 Suzanne held the watch up so we could count the seconds flicking by. I wanted to call the whole thing off, to race back home and pretend that all of this had never happened. I felt guilty, playing so carelessly with my best friend's safety. The five minutes had seemed to take forever, and now I couldn't figure out where all that time had gone. Just before midnight, a branch snapped on the other side of the tracks and Suzanne and I turned to each other, wide-eyed. This new prospect of a danger we had not considered—of something living and breathing and from this world—took me out of the reverie I'd been in. I thought of my mother, frantic and fierce with worry if she were to find my bed empty. The absurdity of what we were doing struck me—calling for a mythic man-beast to hunt us down in the forest? All those disappearances blamed on ghosts, when the world itself was full of danger. I felt, at ten, childish.

My father, I realized, had left us, the way that fathers sometimes did. My skin hummed where it made contact with the clammy night air. I felt exposed, turned inside out. The crater that my father had opened into me shifted slightly—tectonic plates settling after an earthquake.

I don't think I would have screamed if there hadn't been a deadline, but midnight came. At first I just stood there, stunned. But Suzanne nudged me, and I screamed.

I screamed so loudly that I shocked myself. For a moment, I thought someone else had screamed just before I had, and drowned my own noise out. Suzanne let go of my hand and pulled away. She brought her small hands to her ears, and gaped at me. I screamed again, and held it until my voice cracked. I held it until belief in the legend came flooding back to me, until I had blotted out the fact of my father's leaving. I screamed until the woods were smothered by my sound, until they were once again shrouded in myth. Suzanne shook me and shouted, "Let's go!" Her voice was desperate. I took her hand and we dashed into the woods.

We hadn't anticipated how difficult it would be to run while holding hands. We stumbled continuously and tangled our legs. Suzanne's flashlight flickered on and off as she flailed. Sticks and roots we hadn't noticed on the way in tore at our ankles and splintered under the stampede of our frenzied feet. A wind built around us and lapped at our backs. As we fled, I felt the eyes of the beast-man watching us and knew the monster was real. I could sense that his pursuit was leisurely—cruel. We could not outrun him. Suzanne's and my legs caught and we tumbled onto the dirt. Something bit into my knee and our interlocked hands twisted to an odd angle. Still, we did not let go. Suzanne scrambled to her feet, but I simply reared onto my knees. She pulled at me, cartoonish, her feet going through the motions of running.

"Stop," I told her, my hoarse voice not sounding like my own. "Cover your eyes." I climbed slowly to my feet. We were standing in a small clearing where the path forked in several different directions. Shadows from the branches swirled across the ground.

"Listen," I shouted, to the throbbing woods. "I've come to ask you for something."

Suzanne burst into tears. "Please, don't," she sobbed. She stared straight ahead, towards town. Slowly, I turned around, keeping my eyes fixed on the dirt. And there, several yards ahead of me on the path, I saw what I thought were my father's favorite pair of shoes. Before I could think, I snapped my gaze to where my father's face should be. There was nothing: blankness; night; the knotted trunks of impassive trees; a spattering of stars. But a terror filled me. It replaced the air in my lungs with smoke, turned the pit of my stomach cold. I was not moved by what I saw or didn't see, but by the implications of what I'd done. I had looked up. I remembered what my mother had said: she would never have been able keep her eyes averted if she was confronted by the beast. She would be just a pile of bones in the woods. I had not been able to resist, either. I had risked death. I had risked death to save the man who had stepped out over the threshold of our house one morning and emerged a stranger to us, like it was nothing. As if that were a thing that men could do. I had looked up to meet the eyes of evil. I had looked up to catch one last glimpse of a crumbling city. I looked up because I had not, yet, learned to turn my face away from love.

Crybaby Bridge

Sam had been living in Cedar Creek for five months before she discovered it was haunted. Her parents had dragged her to Indiana in August, and now she was spending her last two years of high school surrounded by cornfields in The Lawn Mower Capital of the Midwest. Sam's parents claimed they'd relocated for her mother's new job, but Sam suspected the move had more to do with the trouble she'd been getting into back home in Massachusetts. Cedar Creek didn't seem like a place where there was any trouble to be had. Although the town had a stark, eerie quality to it, Sam wouldn't have guessed that its ordered, sun-streaked streets hid anything sordid or dark or interesting. She assumed its dead were all lying happy and unharassed in their graves.

Sam learned about the hauntings from the girls on her basketball team during the bus ride back from their first away game. The girls, hair slick with sweat, eyes trained on the dark landscape rumbling by, teased each other about the ghosts of Klan members that were rumored to roam the lonely stretch of highway. Sam slid her headphones off and said, "KKK ghosts? That's a story I have to hear." The other girls seemed surprised that Sam had been listening. Sam knew they didn't like her. She wasn't one of them and she wasn't going to pretend otherwise: throw her head back and laugh at their terrible jokes, paint her nails the school colors, drool over the wide-faced dopes on the boys' team, shout 'this is my *jam*' at every song on their warm-up playlist. But they were coming off of a win—a good, hard-fought win—and there was the promise of the Friday night that lay ahead of them, so for a moment there was a sense of camaraderie.

"No, really," Sam said. "I love a good ghost story."

"Then you moved to the right town," Kristen, the team's starting power forward, said.

Cedar Creek had once been home to an asylum for the criminally insane, the site of a natural gas explosion, and the hometown of a serial killer. An undertaker at the cemetery near the train tracks kept the right big toe of every woman he embalmed, so now a swarm of nine-toed ghosts wandered the property. A janitor had hung himself from the pipes in the high school basement, and you could still sometimes hear him struggling with the ropes through the vents. Crybaby Bridge, near the border of Centerville, was haunted by Mad Mary Walcott, who had killed her newborn and then hung herself. At night, a passing motorist or patient thrill seeker might hear the sobs of the drowned child or see a baby's footprints pad across the windshield.

Once Kristen started recounting the stories, the other girls jumped in. They talked over one another in hushed, gleeful tones, adding morbid details or correcting bits of misinformation.

"How do you all know so many stories?" Sam asked. "Is there a ghost guide to Cedar Creek I can get my hands on?"

"We grew up here," Tissy said. "I'm surprised you've taken an interest in the town. I thought you came to Indiana kicking and screaming." Tissy was the team's starting point guard, but Coach Betcher had made it clear that Sam was competition for the spot.

"Trust me, I'm not here by choice," Sam said. "But I'm stuck for another year and a half. I might as well have some fun."

Kristen started to say something, but Tissy threw her a look. They sat in silence until the bus pulled into the high school parking lot.

"I never would've thought Cedar Creek had such an awesome dark side," Sam said to Kristen as they were filing off the bus.

"What do you mean by that?" Tissy asked.

"This place is painfully tame."

"And you must be so fascinating," Tissy said. "Because you have a tongue ring."

"Guess I hit a nerve," Sam said without turning to see Tissy's eyes roll under her perfectly mascaraed lids.

The girls piled off the bus, talking about older brothers who could buy them beer, parents who'd be out late, movies they might watch if nothing else panned out. They avoided looking at Sam. She had a date with Ben, anyway, and she didn't want to be the type of girl they would invite, but in these moments she felt the other girls' pity, which she couldn't stand. She hadn't been popular in Somerville either, but there'd been other girls like her—girls who were on the outside of things and wouldn't want it any other way. Back home, there were friends she knew so well they were like extensions of herself. They would have laughed at these uncomfortable moments with her preppy teammates.

Her parents were waiting to drive her home. Basketball was about the only thing they didn't fight over these days. She slid into the backseat and slammed the door.

"Hey there, MVP," her dad said, putting the car in gear.

Her mom squirmed around in her seat. "What a game! You barely left the court. Coach Betcher must love you."

"She seems to," Sam said. "But she's the only one on the team who does."

"They'll come around."

"I doubt it."

"Maybe if you put in a little more effort. You didn't exactly come in trying to make friends."

"I wish you wouldn't assume everything is *my* fault."

"You don't have to jump down my throat," her mother said. They wound down the field-flanked roads towards the renovated farmhouse that Sam was supposed to call home now.

Her parents had been the supportive and enlightened kind who were always telling her to *just be herself* and encouraging her whims, until *just being herself* stopped meaning obsessions with fantasy books and wearing capes to school, and became having a college boyfriend and skipping classes. Now they didn't know what to do with her.

"I'm going out with Ben tonight," Sam said. "If that's *okay* with you."

Her parents exchanged a nervous look before giving in to the inevitable. If it weren't tonight, it would be another night. Or she could just leave—she'd done that plenty of times before. "As long as you're home by midnight. Not a second later." Sam had made the mistake of telling them Ben's real age: twenty-one. Part of the reason she got in trouble so much was that she hated to lie.

*

Ben lived with his mother and now that it was too cold to be outside, he and Sam had to get creative about where they could be alone. That night, he took her to an unoccupied house that the construction company he worked for was fixing up.

Sam had met him when curiosity pulled her into the model train store in Cedar Creek's town center. She didn't understand how such a place could exist anywhere, nonetheless in a town of seven thousand. She hoped to discover something bizarre: a drug front, or some disheveled shopkeeper who hoarded the trains and couldn't bear to sell any. Ben worked there weekends, doing delicate repairs with tiny tools that looked like medical implements. The way the shop stayed in business was disappointingly simple: most of its business was done online. She'd stayed for hours, talking to Ben about music they both liked, her life back in Massachusetts, his work in the train store, and how lonely he was living with his mother. She'd given him her number before he'd asked.

Ben took her to the top floor of the house, where a small window looked out over a row of rooftops and, beyond that, the inky spreading emptiness of unlit corn and soybean fields. Perhaps the Midwest did offer plenty of opportunities for hauntings, with so much of its land lurking outside the reach of the light.

"Are you sure I can't come to your games?" Ben asked, settling against the bare wall.

"You'd have to deal with my parents, then. And driving an hour to the middle of nowhere just to sit in sweaty gym bleachers isn't an ideal way to spend a Friday evening."

"But I'd get to see you play. I'd cheer you on."

"Rah, rah. Go team."

Ben laughed and kissed her temple. "You know, I can't quite put my finger on why, but you still don't strike me as the high school sports type."

"I'll take that as a compliment," she said, finding his mouth with her own. It puzzled her that he was so ready to claim her, that he would happily sit in the bleachers and yell her name. And he wasn't ashamed to have stuck around this Podunk town; he'd dropped out of Indiana University after a year. But Sam *would* like to see him in the stands and watch Tissy's face cloud with jealousy before she could compose her queenly self. Ben was more attractive than he realized. Sam had seen pictures of him from when he was in high school, before working on houses had bulked him up and he'd grown his beard. His ego hadn't caught up to his appearance, which at least partially explained his devotion to Sam.

Sam pulled him onto the floor. "You're sure?" he asked when she reached for his belt. He asked her this every single time, so she figured he had some lingering discomfort about their age difference. The first time they'd had sex, he'd asked her if she'd ever done it before. "Almost, but not quite," she'd said without thinking, and now she had to live with the lie and the long shadow it was bound to cast. She felt uneasy whenever Jeff, her previous boyfriend, came up in conversation. She suspected Ben would think differently of her if he knew more about that relationship. This was why she hated lying. She wanted to be loved for the person she actually was, or else it was no good.

Afterwards, Ben draped his jacket over them and she rested her head on his wide chest. She loved the little moments of peace after sex almost more than she liked the act. There was no pressure anymore to be clever or impressive. It was like the hours after a hard-won game or a difficult exam: little moments in which to rest.

"Are you glad you moved here?" Ben asked.

"I'm glad I met you," Sam said. "But I hate school and most of the people at school. I'm basically just bored all the time that I'm not with you."

"Even when you're playing basketball?"

"No," Sam admitted.

"What did you do all August, before you met me?"

"Nothing, really. Read, went running, fought with my mom, talked with my friends back home." She'd had no one to spend time with except her parents, who exuded disappointment in her. She'd become obsessed with the fantasy of shedding her skin like a snake. At first, her relationship with Ben was just a way to tip her life from unbearable to slightly bearable. But now she missed him all the time that she wasn't with him.

"Do you believe in ghosts?" she asked.

"Yes," he said without hesitation. "I've seen one. A month after my dad left, I woke up and my grandmother, his mother, was sitting on the edge of my bed. She'd been dead for years."

"That's so creepy."

"I wasn't scared. She was there to comfort me."

"Yes, but from beyond the grave." Sam jabbed him in the ribs.

"Yeah, I guess. Why? Is the attic making you nervous? No one died in the house or anything. It's just for sale."

She explained about the conversation on the bus. It was the first time she'd felt like she had anything interesting to talk about with her teammates.

When midnight came Sam wanted to stay out later, but Ben convinced her to make curfew. This was one of the many ways he was different from Jeff. And better, Sam reminded herself.

*

Sam met Jeff at a party in his dorm at Harvard. He was a genius; in high school he'd built a robot that could perform some sort of surgical operation. He skipped most of his classes, but was acing all his courses anyway. He said he only worked on things that interested him. Sam had interested him. He liked her wildness and that she didn't seem to care what anybody thought of her. He liked that she would try anything new. Sometimes she would leave school at lunch and take the bus to his dorm and find him still asleep at one in the afternoon. Some nights she didn't go home—and what could her parents do? Once, they threatened to get the police involved, but she'd called their bluff.

When she told Jeff that she was pregnant, an eerie calm came over him as he outlined what she had to do and how she had to do it. She saw her first flash of the person he was going to be. She realized that for all his talk about outsiders and weirdos, he was always surrounded by friends and admirers. In three years he would graduate and pass seamlessly into the world and what it expected of him.

Her parents lost it when she told them about the pregnancy, but her mom went with her to get things taken care of. In a way, her parents seemed relieved. They thought this would straighten her out and force her to start *living up to her potential*.

After it was all over, her parents refused to talk about it. They refused to say the word *abortion*. They told her it was better if she didn't tell her friends, but of course she already had. She knew that it was sort of a big deal, but there hadn't even been an operation. She'd been given pills, and there was some stomach pain, and then it had passed and became just something she'd lived through.

A few weeks later Jeff stopped answering her calls. Soon after that her parents announced the move. Then they'd arrived in this flat lonely place and Sam's life had lost all its outlines.

*

A week after that first away game, Coach Betcher persuaded the team to have a sleepover. It would be a way to build stronger relationships, she'd said while looking right at Sam. Sam knew word would get back to Coach if she didn't go, and she wasn't going to give Tissy, who'd offered to host, the satisfaction of her absence.

The evening of the sleepover was bitterly cold, and Tissy's basement felt almost cozy. The first few beers rounded the edges of Sam's resentment. When Tissy's bright-faced mother poked her head down the steps, everyone fumbled to hide the alcohol while Tissy yelled to leave them alone already, and even Sam found this funny.

Then, one of the girls suggested playing Never Have I Ever, a game whose currency was secrets. In response, Tissy said, "I don't think we all know each other well enough."

"What are you talking about?" one of the juniors asked.

"She means me," Sam said. "It's fine. I won't play."

"Then you'll overhear all the dirt on us and we won't learn anything about you. The rest of us practically grew up together. We barely know you."

Sam knew what she did next was important, but she felt like someone had stuffed a cushy towel inside her skull. "Okay. What do you want to know?"

"Let's start with why you think you're so much better than everyone in this town, aside from your cropped hair and your *edgy* music and the fact that you used to ride the subway. You seem to think you're tougher than everyone here. As if we don't also have punks in Indiana."

"Come on, Tissy," Kristen said. "Leave her alone."

"You haven't been through even half of what I have," Sam said.

"Please." Tissy snorted. "Try us."

So Sam told them. She told them about Jeff and his friends. The overdose she'd witnessed. The canister of nitrous oxide they'd stolen from one of the college labs. And she told them about her pregnancy. She told them to shock them and so that they could understand the vast gulf between herself and this silly sleepover. And at least now they could judge her on the decisions she'd actually made.

And the odd thing was, her confession was like flicking a switch. Most of the girls visibly relaxed. They told her that it must have been horrible. They told her that Jeff sounded like a real asshole. They closed ranks around her, as if she was one of them. When no one else was looking she flashed a gloating smile at Tissy.

They stayed up until the beer made it hard for Sam to keep her eyes open. She was surprised to find that she didn't want to sleep. The girls were lying sprawled across the basement floor in sleeping bags and under quilts, with little pockets of low conversation in each corner. Just as Sam was fading, Tissy turned to her and said, "Now I get it, Sam. That's why you were so intrigued by Crybaby Bridge."

Some of the girls sat up, hearing the danger in Tissy's tone. The side conversations stopped. "I understand why you might be especially sympathetic to Mary Walcott, as she searches for her lost daughter."

Kristen hadn't been drinking, so she made the connection before Sam did. "Jesus Christ, Tissy. It's not the same," she said, and the pieces fell into place. Mad Mary, who'd drowned her unwanted child without remorse.

"You think what Mary did and what I did are even comparable?" Sam demanded. Tissy shrugged. "Thanks for reminding me how provincial this place is. Do you even know what *provincial* means?"

Tissy laughed. "You're such a snob."

"We're supposed to be *team-bonding*, remember?" Kristen said. "Not fighting." She got up and switched off the light.

The comparison was ridiculous: taking a pill and bleeding for a few days versus hurling a crying baby into a river. Sam wondered if Tissy was very religious—if she came from a family that picketed Planned Parenthood clinics carrying "abortion is murder" signs. Some of the girls on the team must be. Cedar Creek had more churches than stoplights, and as they'd driven through Ohio, Sam had seen a billboard that said, "Hell is Real," followed by a list of sins. But the other girls had been so nice to her when she'd told them. And Kristen had been so quick to jump to Sam's defense. Sam pulled a pillow over her head and tried to smother the seed of bad feeling that Tissy had planted.

*

Sam napped for most of the next day, so when night finally came she couldn't sleep. She pulled out her laptop and searched for information on Crybaby Bridge. The legend she found was stranger and more elaborate than her teammates had revealed.

Mary Walcott was the youngest sister in a family of modest means. She was always a little unbalanced, and her family didn't allow her to go out very often. Somehow, she met and fell madly in love with a married man—a judge. The two of them started an affair. When she became pregnant, the judge refused to acknowledge the child. After she gave birth, her parents wanted to raise the baby as their own, pretending it was another sister. But Mary didn't want that. She brought the baby to the judge's house and demanded that he leave his wife. She caused enough of a stir that everyone in town learned of the transgression. Her family threw her and the child out on the street and Mary brought the baby to the bridge on Blacklick Road. She drowned the baby and then hung herself from the scaffolding. If she'd had any decency, Mary would have left it at that, with this shameful chapter in the town's history closed. But she didn't.

After her death, she kept on walking the bridge when the night was at its darkest. Her black eyes bulged from her head, and her neck bore a thick scar from where the noose had tightened around it. When cars stopped on her bridge, she banged against the railings and whipped up a nasty wind. Her baby sobbed into the night. Sometimes it sounded as if hundreds of babies were crying out.

The various accounts, like most retellings of legends, did not attempt to understand what Mary had been thinking. They didn't wonder about the night Mary went to confront her lover: whether Mary's heart lurched when she saw the silhouette of the judge's wife peeking out from behind the curtain of an upstairs window. They didn't describe how the anger at this man who'd betrayed her must have grown large in her chest. How the love for him that already lived inside of her didn't make room for this anger, so the two emotions mixed together like different colored fogs. The stories did not consider these things, but Sam did. Sam thought about how Mary must have resented her pretty older sisters. How Mary might have loved the smell of wet leaves by the bridge. Sam wondered whether Mary's last thoughts were of the judge or her baby or her family. Whether she wondered, 'Would my parents take me back, after all, and would I want that?' Or whether her rage pushed everything else aside.

After she closed her computer, Sam lay awake, scared and excited. She didn't care why Tissy had brought it up; Sam was glad she knew the story. She felt, for the first time in a long while, fully alert: aware of herself and her thumping heart. Sound traveled strangely in the new house and from time to time a floorboard would pop or a window would rattle. She fell asleep imagining that she was an explorer, sent to Cedar Creek to discover all its mysteries.

*

That Monday, Sam walked into her first period class and everyone went suddenly quiet. As swiftly as if she'd been punched in the stomach, Sam understood that they knew her secret. And they knew the version that Tissy had spun. Sam kept her eyes locked straight ahead as she slipped into her seat. She didn't bow her head, even as she sensed the whole class watching her. She'd been practicing for this role for years: someone proud and persecuted. Someone who let all the crap the world hurled at her roll off her skin like oil.

At lunch, instead of sitting in the cafeteria with her headphones in and a book in front of her as she normally did, Sam ate her lunch in the gym. Kristen texted her to ask where she was and then appeared at the base of the bleachers.

"I don't know who told first," she said, "but most of the team is on your side. They feel terrible."

"I don't understand why everyone's acting like it's a huge deal. It's not *that* shocking, as far as scandals go." Sam let out a harsh laugh, which the gym swallowed.

"The rumor isn't just that you were pregnant. It's that you bragged about getting an abortion at the sleepover. Tissy is saying you acted as if you were proud of it."

Sam covered her face with her hands, but then quickly took them away so Kristen could see she wasn't crying. "I sort of did, didn't I? God, I'm an idiot."

"*No*," Kristen said. "You just weren't acting ashamed. There's a difference."

But that was bad enough, Sam knew. An indiscretion was forgivable, as long as it was swept under the rug. Mary Walcott's ultimate sin was not the child out of wedlock, but the banging on the judge's door. Her refusal to live the lie they wanted for her.

Sam waited for Kristen's pity or condolences or insistence that *this isn't so bad, really.* But there was only silence, and a slight shift in the bench as Kristen settled next to her.

*

Sam knew that if she could hold the pieces of herself together for a little longer, the whispers in the hallway would pass. She kept her head down at school, did her homework, watched an hour of television with her parents in the evenings, and was fiercer than ever in practice. She talked to Ben on the phone, but he wasn't any help. What could she say to him? *It sucks that everyone in school knows about the time I got pregnant, which might come as a shock to you, since you think I was a virgin when I met you?*

One night Ben showed up at her door with flowers, saying he could tell she was having a bad week. Her mother made a big fuss over putting the flowers in a vase. Ben took Sam for a walk around her neighborhood, gripping her waist. Sam rambled on about an essay she was writing for English class. She arrived home so exhausted she couldn't bring herself to walk upstairs. She fell asleep on the couch and dreamt of Mary's bridge.

Sam had been thinking about the story all week, hunting for records of a real Mary Walcott and reading accounts of sightings. In her dream, Mary was wearing a hooded cloak. The skin on her face was cracked and pale. Her eyelashes were long and crumpled like spider legs. She looked like she wanted to tell Sam something. Mary opened her mouth as if to reveal an important truth, but instead a scream exploded from the ghost's lips and Sam started awake. Her parents had covered her with a blanket while she slept. She imagined them standing over her, thinking she was finally starting to settle down: doing her homework, dating a boy who brought her flowers. *She's doing so well,* Sam imagined her mother whispering to her father. *And look how sweet she looks, asleep.* This false belief in her was worse than their disappointment, worse than the worst fights she'd ever had with them.

*

The next day, as the team was milling around after practice, Sam overheard a few of the upperclassmen talking about going to the movies. When Kristen saw that Sam was listening, she invited her.

"I think I'll sit this one out," Sam said.

"It'll be fun," Kristen said. "You can ride with me."

"Thanks, but I'm seeing Ben tonight, anyway. I should go home and get ready."

"Maybe you could bring him?"

"Another time."

"You've got more exciting plans than us?" Tissy asked.

Sam rooted around in her gym bag to hide her angry blush. She hadn't been able to look Tissy in the face since the rumor had spread—not because she felt betrayed, but because Tissy had bested her. She wasn't about to admit that her big plan for the evening was to watch television with Ben and his mom. She straightened up and said, "Actually, my boyfriend's taking me to Crybaby Bridge. We're going ghost hunting."

Tissy didn't know how to respond, which Sam counted as a small victory.

"That's awesome," Kristen said. "Promise me you'll report back. If you see or *hear* anything, you need to text us right away."

Sam nodded, wiping the sweat from her forehead with the bottom of her jersey.

Tissy paused at the locker room door. "I think you might have some luck. If anyone can channel Mary, I imagine it would be you."

"You ignorant townie bitch." The rest of the team stopped shuffling with their bags and stared. "Your stupid hick ghost stories don't scare me."

"So there it is. She thinks we're all hicks."

"I said *you* were a hick. If you hate me so much, stop dancing around it and say so already."

"Fine. I hate you," Tissy said.

*

Ben was hesitant to go to the bridge, but after a little persuading he seemed excited. Sam was eager to head out. When she got into Ben's car, her teeth were chattering, and she didn't think it was only from the cold. A nervous energy had been knocking around inside her all week and the shaking seemed like a way to let it out. When they reached the main crossroad, Ben headed towards an area of town Sam had never been to.

"Are you finally going to tell me what's been going on with you this week?" he asked. "You've been acting really off."

"School's been tense."

"I know *something* happened. Things were getting better—you were even saying nice things about the girls on your team."

"I was being naïve. I'm never going to fit in here. I'm always going to be the weird new girl." The road narrowed and the streetlights were few and far between. Ben flicked his brights on.

"Five months is a long time to be the new girl," he said. "You might want to start letting your guard down a bit."

"You don't know these girls or what they're like. You don't know what I'm dealing with."

"I sort of do. Things can't have changed that much in four years. I just mean that you're clearly capable of being wonderful. Why don't you act around them the way you act around me?"

"How do you know I don't?" Sam said, but then she thought it over. "I don't know."

Ben put a hand on her knee. "Tonight should take your mind off it."

"That's the idea." Sam looked past Ben at the darkness that thickened as it spread away from the road. She wasn't used to such vast empty spaces. The fields seemed to stretch forever, as if she were looking out across the ocean.

When they reached the bridge, Ben stopped the car and asked, "You ready?" Sam could make out the rusty railings illuminated in the headlights. She searched for movement in the gloom.

"Are you sure the bridge is safe?" Sam asked. "To drive over?"

"Are you having doubts, my fearless leader?"

Sam laughed. "I'm not the doubting kind."

The car lurched and then crept onto the bridge. Sam listened to the tires gripping the gravel and the water running underneath them. Ben cut the lights. Sam couldn't remember ever being in such complete blackness. She couldn't even see Ben. The corroded railings disappeared. The sparse trees at the bank of the creek disappeared. The narrow cracking road disappeared. Only the sky, pin-pricked with light, remained.

Sam put her arm through Ben's and squeezed. This was the moment she'd been searching for: two people pulled together against the harsh night. She wanted the intimacy of confronting something unfamiliar together, of having a moment so out of the ordinary they both were bound to remember it forever.

Ben rolled down the windows. "Listen," he said. "Do you hear something moving?"

Sam could hear the low humming of the car motor and the trees creaking. She heard a splash somewhere beside her and shivered at the whorls of cold air drifting through the open windows. And maybe, under the rest of the noises, she heard movement on the bank. "Turn the car off," she said. "So we can hear."

"But what if we have to make a quick getaway?" He pulled the keys out of the ignition.

"Are you trying to freak me out?" Sam kissed his shoulder.

And then the sound of sobbing rose from the riverbanks. It started on their right, before a chorus of cries joined in on the left. "Oh, my God," Ben said. "What the hell?" He fumbled with the keys, but Sam stopped him. This was what they'd come here for. If they left, they'd always wonder.

The crying increased in volume. Sam had heard that coyotes could sound like women screaming. Or maybe that was wolves.

She was so quick to try to rationalize it. She hadn't really expected to experience anything supernatural, but why not? The stories must come from somewhere.

Bits of laughter cut through the noise. Sam exhaled slowly. She heard choked whispering. "Relax," she said to Ben, who was craning his neck out the window. "It's just a trick."

"What the hell kind of trick is this?"

"It's the girls on my team. I told them we were coming." Her eyes were adjusting, and she was surprised to find how well she could see in what she'd first perceived as total darkness. She could see Ben clearly now. He looked older, with parts of his face thrown into shadow. She could make out the shape of the metal girders and the white line marking the side of the road. She could even see the slow, erratic swaying of the trees.

A scream rose from the bank and Sam jumped. She forced herself to laugh, but the sound came out more like a cough. "All right, assholes," she yelled. "Nice try." She reached for the handle, but couldn't bring herself to open the door.

There was a ping as something struck the side of the bridge. Then something flew over the railing and hit the car. Rocks and sticks and pebbles bounced across the pavement, sounding like rain on a skylight. Something thumped against the car door. "Cut it out," Sam shouted. "The joke's over. I know it's you guys."

Someone made an exaggerated hooting sound, like a cartoon ghost, and the group erupted in giggles. "Help me, Mommy. Don't do it!"

"That's enough," someone hissed, and Sam felt a stab of anger when she realized it was Kristen.

"What the hell, Kristen?" she shouted.

After a beat, Kristen called, "We're just messing around."

"No," Sam said softly, just to Ben. "They did this to scare the shit out of me. Because they're horrible."

"Probably it's just, like, a sort of hazing?" Ben was trying to reassure her, but there was more question than statement in his voice.

"This is even meaner than it seems," Sam said.

Ben started to say something and then stopped.

"What?"

"I just don't understand. Why do they hate you so much?"

Sam was afraid that if she tried to answer, she'd start crying. "Take me home," she said.

Ben didn't make any move to turn on the car. "Maybe you should talk to them," he said. "Show them there are no hard feelings."

But all she had were hard feelings. She stepped out of the car. "The fun's over. Come up here and fucking talk to me."

Sam heard the girls climbing up the riverbank and the splash of upturned rocks rolling into the water. "You have to admit, we got you pretty good," Mel said, when they'd made the trek up to where Sam was standing.

"And really, the joke's on us," Kristen said. "We've been sitting here freezing for the past hour."

"What in the fuck is wrong with you?" Sam said. She turned to Tissy. "How could you think that what I did is anything like what Mary did?"

"That's not what we meant," Kristen said. "Really."

"That's why she came up with the idea," Sam said, gesturing to Tissy, who shrugged, as if she couldn't be bothered to confirm or deny.

"What's going on?" Ben said, climbing out of the car. "I'm missing something."

No one would meet his eyes.

Then Tissy said, "Sam claimed she hadn't cried in ten years, but I thought she was lying. I wanted to see if we could scare her enough to make her cry."

Ben looked from Tissy back to Sam.

"Get it?" Tissy said. "*Crybaby* Bridge."

"Okay," Ben said, leaning against the car. "Well, I guess it'll take more than that. You definitely scared the shit out of me, but she's dry-eyed."

"She's lying," Sam said. "Right before I moved here, I had an abortion."

Ben laughed weakly, but he caught on before he made the mistake of saying that that was impossible.

"Get it?" Sam said. "Cry*baby* Bridge."

"It really wasn't like that," Mel said, and a few of the other girls chimed in.

"I'm sorry," Sam said to Ben.

"I just don't understand." Ben ran his hand through his hair and studied the trees behind Sam's teammates.

"I wanted to tell you, but I didn't know how you'd react."

But Ben wasn't paying attention to her. He was focused on the other side of the bridge. "What *is* that?" he said.

They all turned in unison to see what he was staring at. There was an old woman watching them. She held a bundle in her arms, but she was too far away for Sam to see her clearly.

"Is this part of the joke?" Sam asked.

"No," Kristen said. "Who is that?"

The woman began to move towards them with awkward lurching steps. Ben clambered into the car, accidentally striking the horn. The woman stopped and turned to face the noise. "Get in," he whispered. The woman was only about ten yards away. "Oh, God, what is that?" He leaned forward and squinted.

The woman began creeping forward again. Ben fumbled with the keys and tried to jam them into the ignition. "Get in!" he yelled and then pulled Sam onto his lap. She scrambled over him into the passenger seat, and then leaned out the open window. The woman approached the car. She had long black hair and bruised eyes. As she got closer, Sam was less sure of her age; it was hard to tell what were wrinkles and what were shadows. The woman looked confused and angry. The bundle in her arms squirmed and the face of a small brown dog appeared from the cloth. Sam screamed and the car jumped to life. Ben threw it in gear and backed off the bridge. The other girls were sprinting towards two cars parked in the high grasses next to the road.

"Wait," Sam said, turning to catch another glimpse of the woman. "Ben, wait!"

Ben veered off the road so he could whip the car around. The wheels spun in place and then jerked forward. "Is she following?" Ben gasped.

"Stop," Sam said. She tried to open the door but Ben sped up. Sam wrenched around and watched the woman fade to nothingness.

Her teammates' cars were still dark. They were probably frantically searching for keys, unlocking doors, clutching each other. Sam wondered what the woman would do to them if she reached them. Sam didn't like where her thoughts went from there: the woman's hands scratching at their pretty faces; the woman dragging the girls back to the bridge and holding their heads underwater until they stopped jerking. Sam didn't like that she wanted this.

Ben was breathing heavily, and his eyes were wide and unfocused. Freezing air rushed through the car. Sam motioned to his window and he rolled it up.

"That couldn't have been a ghost," he said. "I know what you're thinking, but that wasn't Mary."

"How else do you explain it? You *saw* her."

"It must have been one of your friends, dressed up or something."

"I don't think so," Sam said. "Did you see how scared they were?"

"You're being ridiculous."

"You said you've seen a ghost before."

"That was different. This is just a made-up legend. There never was any real Mary Walcott. No one actually drowned her child in the river."

"Why not?" Sam said. "That kind of thing happens."

Ben shook his head. "Maybe we should call the police. Maybe it was an old woman who was lost or something. Maybe she needed our help."

"You believed the ghost story enough to take me."

"If I believed it was real, I *never* would've taken you."

Cornstalks raced by Sam's window, looking like waves rolling across the surface of a tremendous ocean.

"Do you want to go somewhere?" Ben asked.

"I want to go home." If only Sam could have a moment to catch her breath, to stop running from whatever was chasing her and just let it hit her. The car turned onto a road she recognized.

"Once you've calmed down, we need to talk," Ben said.

"If you want to break up with me, that's fine."

"Don't make me the bad guy," he said. Then his voice grew almost tender. "So you really did that?"

Sam nodded.

"And you've been lying to me about it for months?"

"I didn't know what you'd think. After all, you're a good Christian boy."

"That's not fair. You can't really think of me as just that. Can you?"

"Well. How do you feel about it?" Sam wouldn't look at Ben. In the pocket of silence before his answer, she watched the headlights catch the green eyes of a raccoon.

"It's not the choice I would have made."

Anger flared through Sam's whole body. "You'd never have to make it."

"No, but I can understand. I'm not saying you shouldn't have done it. I'm saying *I* wouldn't have."

"That's the problem with everyone. You all seem to think you can understand."

"*Sam*," Ben said. "I'm not the bad guy."

"Right, because I am. Go to hell. Or does the phrase offend you?"

"You've *hurt* me." Ben's voice faltered. "I thought you were a different sort of person than you are."

"What kind of person am I?" Sam asked. When he didn't respond, she added, "At least this was fun while it lasted."

"We should keep talking about this," Ben said.

"Don't worry. You can just be done with me."

Ben drove down her family's long driveway and put the car in park. The porch light was off. Ben was shaking a little, maybe crying.

Sam leaned back and closed her eyes. An image of the woman's desperate, lined face appeared. Sam snapped her head forward and gripped the door handle. "It *was* Mary Walcott," she said, suddenly sure. "I hope she finds you. I hope she comes for you tonight."

She climbed out of the car. The way was lit by Ben's headlights. She stopped with her hand on the cold doorknob, the strange new sounds of the field whirring around her. She knew that even after all that she'd done to him, Ben would wait until she was inside. Her anger left her, and she wondered how to face the days, the weeks, the months ahead.

*

When she stepped inside, she gasped. But it was only her mother, nodding off over a book.

"The porch light went out. I wanted to make sure you got home. Are you all right?"

Sam watched Ben's headlights recede. "How does someone know if they're a bad person?" she asked.

Her mother took off her reading glasses, considered. "They never think to ask questions like that."

Sam began to cry. She went to her mother, who'd forced Sam into this unfamiliar town and uprooted her when she'd most needed to put down roots. Who'd only wanted to keep Sam safe.

"Honey," her mother said. "What's wrong?"

"You made me feel so ashamed," Sam said.

"I didn't know what to do," her mother said, with no need for clarification. "I was scared."

Sam rested her head in her mother's lap. "But I'm not ashamed," she said. "I'm not."

Outside, the frozen brush snapped as some creature slunk by the house, making its nightly rounds. If Sam had gone to the window, she wouldn't have been able to make out shapes in the dark. Anything could have been out there.

The Last Unmapped Places

Imagine, please, a September storm hugging the coast as it sweeps northward. Dark, moody skies with clouds so thick they seem solid. The apple trees in our backyard thrashing. A heavy blue tarp, draped over whatever project my dad was working on at the time, loose and flapping in the wind. The ocean, only a few miles from our house, roiling along the jagged shoreline. The rain arriving all in one rush like an exhaled breath. My family inside, snug and languid and unaware of my absence. My mother stretched across the couch, reading; my father in the kitchen pickling vegetables; my twin sister drawing quietly at the coffee table. A crack of thunder so loud and so in sync with the lightning flash that my mother is about to say, *That must have struck something nearby.* She stops because my sister's hair is standing on end, fanned out like a sea anemone. Then my mother smells singed wood, singed earth, singed hair. Hannah is crying and my mother grabs her, but Hannah appears to be uninjured. My father rushes into the living room, knife still in hand. "What happened? Why is she screaming?" My mother smooths down Hannah's hair and asks her what hurts. Hannah continues to sob. "Oh my god," my mother says when she realizes there's nothing wrong with this twin, the one safe in the living room with her and my father. "Oh my god. Where's Rachael?"

Hannah and I were eight at the time. I was outside by the backyard oak tree. The lightning cored the oak and then an errant arm of electricity reached for me. I was out cold for several minutes and when I opened my eyes the world swam in front of me like a television channel that wasn't in focus. Thanks to the miracle of Hannah's electrically charged hair, my parents were there when I woke and an ambulance was already wailing in the distance. My mother loves this story. As family lore it's irresistible: the raging storm, the twin connection, my mother's instincts, the proof of our uniqueness, and the razor's edge of disaster that only nicked us.

I spent a week in the hospital. For several years I had joint pain and occasional seizures in which my face went slack and my head snapped up and down like a skipping CD. I started getting migraines accompanied by blurred vision and moving colors and a strange settled sense of dread. But I was lucky to survive. The doctors and nurses told me so again and again. Still, I didn't feel lucky. I felt exposed. I felt like someone had broken into the house that was my body and moved all my things around.

And the part of the story that my mother always left out of her frequent retellings: when my parents asked if I remembered anything leading up to the lightning strike, I told them that I had been beckoned outside by a man in a black rain cape. His voice was low and throaty. His breath smelled like damp soil. When he gestured for me to walk in front of him and his cape opened, I saw that his arm was webbed; a pink flap of flesh ran from his wrist to his waist. His shoulders were high and hunched. I wanted to resist, but was too scared of not obeying. Rainwater streamed over his face. He told me, "The smoke gets thicker the further you go."

*

We lived in a small town on the Maine coast, where kids rode dirt bikes through the woods and walked without hesitation over barely frozen streams and had no fear of the dark, yawning nights that seemed to swallow everything during our long winters. Even before the lightning strike, I was the quieter, stranger twin. Afterwards, I grew jumpy and fearful, which were great sins in our town's childhood kingdom. Hannah saved me from being an outcast. Whenever she sensed I was about to do or say something too weird she changed the subject or caught my eye and gave a quick shake of her head. When I told friends at a sleepover to keep the lamp on to ward off the Webbed-Arm Man, Hannah laughed loudly and said he was just a character from a bedtime story our mom had told us. When I hesitated to retrieve a Frisbee from a crawl space that pulsed with a sinister energy or a beach ball that floated too far from the shore, Hannah would rush past me with feigned excitement and recover the item before I could refuse.

In some fundamental way, I didn't understand what people expected of me. Once, when I was ten, I proudly showed the supermarket cashier a dead mouse that our cat had killed. I'd been keeping it in a toy handbag. As the cashier shrieked and people in line turned away, my mother said only, "She's a little scientist, this one!" while Hannah apologized and ushered me out the door. My mother, a librarian from New York with wild gray hair that she wore much longer than was fashionable, wasn't perturbed by my behavior or the way the town regarded me. But my father was horrified when Mom recounted the story. He buried the mouse, still in the handbag, in the yard while I cried. Dad asked Hannah what I'd been thinking and Hannah said, "She wanted it for her bone collection," reluctantly leading him to where I'd stored the sun-bleached skeleton of an opossum I'd found by our back fence.

Hannah was my opposite in every way. She resembled our dad: sandy-haired, athletic, and approachable. I'm more like our mother: dark-eyed with angular features and unruly curls. And Hannah always knew exactly what people expected of her, which was a different sort of burden than the one I carried. She was adored, confided in, and admired, but she had her own anxieties, which she hid from everyone but me. She worried about our father, who she claimed was stressed about money and the properties he managed. She worried that our mother found us boring. She worried about our parents' frequent arguments, about a close friend whose brother was cruel, and I assume also about me—my fixations, my strangeness, my poor health.

I never figured out how Hannah intuited others' secrets, but even when she told me about them, they didn't trouble me much. My fears were visceral: that the undercurrent would drag me to sea if I went into the ocean past my knees; that our dad's truck would fishtail in the snow on the drive to school; that there was someone crouching behind the rhododendron bush, ready to grab me every time I rushed onto the porch. I had seen the Webbed-Arm Man and I knew he was watching from whatever dusky corner of the universe he resided in. I knew that he was waiting.

*

Before we go any further: Hannah is dead. She drowned three years ago, when we were thirty-one. The knowledge of her death is like the fear I felt in childhood: a second shadow that's always with me. And this shadow falls heavily over my recollections of our lives, so there's no true way to tell this story if you don't know that's what I'm building towards. Besides, I've never liked surprises, even when they're for other people.

*

Hannah and I never stopped being close, though eventually the world began to edge its way in. Amidst the many other mild mortifications of middle school, Hannah began to cultivate friendships that, for the first time, didn't include me. In high school, she joined the volleyball team and jogged five miles every morning before breakfast. As I brushed my teeth, I would watch from the small bathroom window as she stretched in the driveway, lithe and flushed and pleased with how much she'd accomplished while the neighbors still slept. I had no talent for sports, but I developed an intense passion for geology and started a blog on the rock formations of the Maine coast. Hannah had her first boyfriend, a surprisingly tame relationship that nonetheless overwhelmed her and filled her with moony longing. But weekday evenings still found us in comfortable camaraderie in our room, debriefing the day and planning for the next one.

On our sixteenth birthday, Hannah secured her license and we discovered how much we loved to drive together. We'd meander through the woods, pointing out abandoned railroad crossings, fire towers, and leaning cabins. I felt more settled than I had in childhood, tethered more firmly to the world as others saw it, but I had few friends and I was achingly lonely when Hannah disappeared to parties or team sleepovers or her boyfriend's basement on weekend evenings.

When the time came to apply to college, our dad sat us down at the kitchen table and told us he wanted us to go to different schools. Hannah laughed and said we'd consider it. Later, I asked Hannah what the big fuss was and she told me, "He wants us to be normal," which was how I learned he thought we weren't.

*

We disregarded Dad's advice and went to a small college within an hour's drive of our hometown. Everything about college was a surprise. I, who'd never felt comfortable anywhere, was suddenly full of purpose. I dove with pleasure into the study of maritime history, the geology of the ocean floor, cartography in the middle ages. It seemed there was a class for everything. I even braved late-night walks alone through the dark campus, grasses rustling and strangers' footsteps echoing through the narrow corridors between buildings, if it meant I could stay at the college's library until it closed. I started dating a girl who worked in the interlibrary loan office and was absorbed into her group of clove-smoking, intricately tattooed friends. I took six classes at a time. I helped my professors with their research. I never turned in a single assignment late, even when my migraines nestled in my head and pulsed their jagged spikes into the tender flesh behind my eyes.

Hannah, who'd always been competent and sure-footed, suddenly lost all momentum. She'd been recruited for volleyball, but played badly and was taken off the starting line-up. Eventually, she quit the team. She began drinking more and slept with her Spanish TA. When she confessed to her chaste high school sweetheart, he refused to forgive her.

She missed classes because she'd been partying, then because she just didn't want to go. She chose subjects seemingly at random. She began staging protests with my girlfriend's friends, becoming passionate about specific causes—veganism, the cafeteria workers' rights, banning plastic containers—only to abandon them weeks later. She started a frenzy of volunteering—teaching ELL courses to custodial staff at the school, serving at the town's soup kitchen, working with kids at a youth shelter.

When we were juniors, our parents divorced. I knew I should have felt more strongly about it, but all I felt was a slight sadness at the thought of our dad all alone in our old house. Hannah, on the other hand, spent hours on the phone trying to reconcile them, reckoning with my mother's anger and restlessness, my father's loneliness and sense of failure. Against the advice of her advisor, she went abroad to Madrid. My migraines became unbearable while she was gone and I was so exhausted I starting falling asleep in class. I didn't think I'd survive her absence, but after only a month, Hannah had an incident with some sleeping pills and red wine that alarmed her host family, and it was decided she'd come back early. When I picked her up at the airport, she was so thin I wanted to wrap my arms around her just to give her more heft. On the ride home she told me, "It's like I'm watching myself. I don't even know who's running the show." She moved in with me and for a time we were as close as we'd ever been. I walked her through her daily routines until she'd regained her bearings and come back into herself.

Our senior year, I got lost in my thesis, a sprawling history of humans' attempt to map the seafloor, and my girlfriend felt neglected and left me for a freshman poet. Hannah's charm and intelligence kept her held aloft while she continued to slip and slide, never quite gaining traction. She came home one night, unsteadily drunk, and darkened when she saw me with a draft of my thesis spread across the floor. "Look at you," she said to me. "You're so good. You're so focused. Do you remember when I had to check the closet every night for the Webbed-Arm Man before you could sleep?"

"You saved me," I told her.

"Rachael," she said, dropping to her knees in front of me, grasping my wrists. "How does a person know what they're worth?"

When she touched me, the boundary between us fell away, as it often had when we were children. I felt her shame and emptiness like a wave of nausea. I felt her furious love for the world and her belief that she was undeserving of it. I realized that her frenzy of volunteer work was her way of trying to earn her place—not just at the college, but on this earth. I rested my forehead against hers. She *had* saved me; she was still saving me. "There's no one better than you," I told her, because it was true.

*

Hannah's mention of the Webbed-Arm Man that night surprised me. Over the years, we'd stopped discussing him, and I thought she'd mostly forgotten him. I had not. My fear of him had lost its sharp edge, but I never stopped believing. I'd seen or sensed him several other times. When I had my seizures, I used to wake to the harsh smell of wood smoke, which I took as a signal that the Webbed-Arm Man was close. When I was twelve, an October snowstorm knocked out the power and Mom sent me to retrieve a flashlight. The candle I was holding snuffed out just as I took my first step onto the basement staircase. I reached an exploratory hand into the sudden blackness and felt a wet flap of flesh; I scrambled back upstairs and locked the door behind me. I also occasionally caught glimpses of him under porches or in bushes or off the side of the road. And once, when I was brushing my teeth in high school, worrying over why Hannah hadn't yet returned from her morning run, I saw him leaning against our neighbor's fence, his eyes also trained down the road. By the time I'd gained enough courage to rush outside, he was gone and I could see Hannah turning onto our street. My dad dismissed my sightings as the product of an overactive imagination or a symptom of my epilepsy. My mother believed me, or claims she did.

Even in college, when I'd become less skittish and more grounded, he was present in my life. Most notably, on a camping trip at Acadia National Park with my girlfriend, I'd made the Webbed-Arm Man into a campfire tale as we roasted marshmallows, embellishing the story with a series of elaborate recurring nightmares I'd never had. That night I couldn't sleep, worrying about a group of men at the site next to ours, who'd kept trying to flirt with us and then grown surly and quiet when they realized we were a couple. It began to rain and the loamy smell of the wet soil brought the Webbed-Arm Man back to me in the form I always knew him to be: a memory and not an invention. I woke up Elise and forced her to sleep in the locked car with me. When we drove into Bar Harbor the next morning, I had a voicemail from Hannah.

"I know, I know, I *know* you're fine," the recording said. "But I just had a feeling I couldn't shake, so please call me when you're back in civilization, okay?"

*

For me, the years after college passed like rolling down a hill: effortless and inevitable. I attended grad school, where a tendency towards fixation is the most promising trait, and my research burned so brightly everything else in my life seemed to dim. I won awards. I graduated with the highest honors and started my dream job as a map librarian at the Boston Public Library. A woman named Priya took an interest in me after touring an exhibit I'd curated on mapping the cosmos, and fought her way into my vision long enough to make herself part of my routine.

Hannah took back up with her high school boyfriend and they were married within a year. Part of the reason he'd been so chaste and unforgiving all those years ago was because he was a deeply, onerously religious man. Hannah became very involved in their church, which distressed Mom to no end. But the church stabilized Hannah's life and gave her a community who valued her generosity, even if they couldn't see that it wasn't earnestly in service to the lord, but born from her intense need to correct the debt she thought she owed the world. Out of some punishing instinct, she got a job organizing study abroad programs at a company based in Portland, which she was very good at despite her failure in Madrid.

Although our lives had very different shapes, she remained one of the only people whose motivations and desires were not opaque to me. Every morning we woke an hour early so we could talk on the phone as we drank our coffee. I'd close my eyes and imagine her across from me, and it always seemed that if I just reached out my arm, she'd be there on the other side of the table, ready to take my hand. Once, when I opened my eyes after the call, I was looking at Hannah and Chris's tidy kitchen counter and had to shake my head hard before my own small apartment came back into view.

*

I remember almost everything about the night that Hannah died. I'd brought Priya to Maine for Thanksgiving to meet my family. Priya is Indian-Canadian, so she had no other plans, and she wanted to see where I came from and get to know the golden sister I talked so much about. Hannah and Chris picked us up at the train station and whisked us to Mom's apartment in Portland for our day-before-Thanksgiving meal, which Mom kept calling "the first Thanksgiving" to acknowledge that we were going to our father's the next day.

By then, my mother had moved into an attic apartment at the edge of the city. The house was at the top of a steep hill and Mom's bedroom window had an expansive view of the bay, so in the mornings she could watch the lobster boats slinking out to sea and the clouds of greedy seagulls trailing after them. Hannah was worried that Mom was becoming eccentric—she'd developed an obsession with the Canadian folk artist Maud Lewis and painted bright pastoral scenes on every free surface of her apartment—but Mom was much happier than she'd ever been living with Dad or raising us.

Priya complimented my mother's artwork and seemed genuinely charmed that Mom had ordered a buffet of Thai take-out because she'd forgotten to defrost the turkey. Mom offered to show Priya more of her paintings after dinner. I watched Hannah's expression carefully for a clue as to how the interaction was going. Hannah gave me a little nod of approval, but there was sadness underneath it.

After dinner, Mom disappeared into the kitchen and reappeared with a pot of mulled wine. When she theatrically took off the lid, the dining room filled with the scent of cloves and Priya clapped. Mom bowed and then poured each of us a steaming mugful. When she slid one over to Chris, he said stiffly, "You know I can't have that." He was five years sober.

"Just one can't hurt!" My mother took a showy sip of hers. "It's delicious."

"She does this on purpose," Chris said to Hannah. He hated when anyone drew attention to his sobriety, highlighting his one deviation from the righteous path.

Hannah took his mug and put it next to her own. She said something softly to him that I couldn't quite make out.

"Suit yourself," Mom said. "But it's the one thing I cooked tonight." She laughed. When no one laughed with her she shrugged. "I guess if *you're* drinking, Hannah, that means no luck yet on the pregnancy front."

Hannah blushed and shook her head. She and Chris had been trying for years. Chris insisted that God would bless them when it was time.

"My friend Patty was telling me all about IVF," Mom said. "It's normal now. So there's no need to be so prudish about it."

"That's enough!" Chris said, so loudly that Priya jumped.

"Don't be startled, dear," Mom said. "He's always like this. You two have the right idea. If I'd been smarter, I'd have been a lesbian, too."

"Mom," Hannah said sharply. She turned to me, "How's your new exhibit coming? Have you started installing it yet?"

"What new exhibit?" Mom asked, allowing herself to be led. "Why didn't you tell me about it?"

"I did," I said. "When we talked last month." But Mom only vaguely remembered the conversation—she was often painting or out for a walk when we talked on the phone. But I was happy to explain the project again; my work is one of the few conversation topics that come easily to me.

This was the first major exhibit I was designing on my own. It focused on places that are still uncharted. I'd titled it *The Last Unmapped Places*, and was working sixty-hour weeks because I needed it to be perfect.

Mom asked for examples, and I explained about the miles-deep cave system under farmland in Vietnam, an unclimbed mountain in Bhutan, the shifting outline of Greenland's coast, and shantytowns in Pakistan with no reliable street maps.

Hannah had finished both her and Chris's wine and was filling her mug again. Chris made a show of checking his watch. "You're sure you want to have another?"

I kept talking as if he hadn't interrupted, so Hannah wouldn't have to respond. "The challenge is figuring out what to display, since the focus is the *un*mapped. But really, it's about mystery and its tug on the imagination. Our last exhibit was on *trains*, and now we get to feature remote sections of the Amazon jungle seen by no one still alive on this earth."

"How ambitious," Chris said, draping his arm over the back of Hannah's chair in the proprietary posture that men like him are made for. "But you should be careful. If you spend too much time scratching away at the mystery, you'll eliminate the very thing you think you love. As soon as you find the unknown, it becomes the known."

"Is this about God?" I said. "Again?"

"Rachael," Hannah said. "He's not trying to convert you. He's just making conversation."

"He wants to make good believers out of all of us, like he did with you."

Priya put a cautionary hand on my knee.

"I don't have to tolerate this," Chris said.

"She's just feeling defensive," Hannah murmured.

"Don't do this again," Chris said. "Pick a side."

"How can I?"

Chris stood, nearly upturning Mom's wobbly table when he braced himself against it. "I'm going home. If you want to stay, you can call me when you need a ride."

"Don't be so dramatic," I said, but I was pleased that the night would carry on without him.

"So you're really not coming?" he asked. Hannah didn't look at him when she shook her head.

We continued drinking, and I began to feel really good, surrounded by the women who made up the whole of my social world. At some point, Mom announced that she was going to bed, but encouraged us to stay up talking.

After she left, Hannah became confessional with Priya. She explained that we hadn't been raised with God. She was drunk—really drunk, like I hadn't seen since college. "I do feel awe in church," she said. "But the God I feel, it's as if He's channeled through Chris, like I'm believing *through* him."

"There's nothing wrong with that," Priya said. I could tell she liked Hannah, which was not a surprise. Everyone liked Hannah.

"Do you think it's really okay? Sometimes I don't know." Hannah started to cry. Priya and I got out of our seats and crouched next to her. We each took one of her hands.

When Hannah's crying had slowed she said, "I'm not always like this." Then, she turned to me and said, "I don't know what's happening to me. I feel like I don't have any edges anymore. The way I used to feel only with you, I feel that way with everyone."

I squeezed her hand.

I don't remember what we talked about after that strange interlude, but we forged on and the mood lightened. Eventually Priya said that she'd like to see Maine's famous coastline before she left, and Hannah said, "What better time than now?"

Outside, the night was clear and fresh and ripe, and it calmed me to take the sharp air into my lungs. Hannah led us to a park with a small gazebo and a wrought-iron fence. It was an almost-full moon; a funnel of light sliced across the river. We climbed down a steep stone staircase partially hidden by trees, which spilled out onto a paved path that wrapped around the cliff. I recovered my bearings; if we'd gone right we would have come across the ferry terminal and then the seafood restaurants and ice cream shops and fish markets. Instead, we turned left, towards the open ocean. We could hear waves slapping against the sea wall.

Priya took in a big breath. "I smell salt!" she said, delighted.

"The water's so choppy." I was surprised. "It's not that windy."

"Are you already forgetting the ways of the ocean?" Hannah teased. "It stormed yesterday. The sea remembers."

When we came to an old jetty, Priya hopped out onto the rocks. She took in the gyrating peaks and valleys of the water. "It's so beautiful," she said. "On a night like this, it's obvious there's no risk of losing mystery, no matter how much you study it."

Hannah followed Priya onto the rocks. "How lovely," she said. "What a lovely sentiment." Then she said, so low that I could barely hear her over the tut-tut of the waves, "You will be so good for Rachael."

And then something went wrong. A twisted ankle, the sole of a shoe too smooth to grip the rock face, or a step made unstable with alcohol. Or maybe something darker. I know. I know there's the possibility that Hannah intended, or half-intended, to go in. The only certainty is that one moment Hannah was a striking silhouette against the blue-black sky, and the next she was in the water.

I heard the splash and the sickening intake of breath as the cold hit her. I screamed. I ran to the sea wall and dropped to my knees. I searched and found Hannah surfacing, pulled in toward the piers faster than I would have expected. She tore at the water.

I must have encouraged Hannah to swim. I must have shouted for help. Hannah, when she said something finally, was impossible to understand.

I stood up. I took off my shoes and my coat. From the jetty, Priya saw my intent and hissed with as much intensity as a slap, "Don't you dare."

Still, I took a step back, poised to jump. I felt how cold the ground was beneath my socked feet, which made me pause for only a moment, but it was enough time for Hannah to go under again. I lost her. I scanned the water, then caught sight of a dark figure. I wasn't sure if I was seeing a shadow or an underwater rock or her body. "Do you see her?" I demanded. Priya was useless, sobbing and shaking.

Then, around the edges of the Hannah-shaped blot, I saw a black, shifting form that slithered through the water like heavy fog. The shadow slunk forward, somewhere between a liquid and a solid, before coming together and opening its great webbed arms behind her. The air grew thick and murky and there was a sudden dank-earth smell. There is no way for me to describe it now—it's like describing the particular smell of a house you no longer live in—as clear and distinct as a fingerprint but you only know it when it's around you. I'd smelled it before, all those years ago. The fear I felt was beyond fear. It was fear that the bottom fell off of.

Later, after Priya's desperate call to the police, and the officers' embarrassed questions, and the rescue boat and the divers and the condescending explanations about currents and riverbeds and tides, I asked Priya if she saw the thing in the water, the thing that wrapped its arms around Hannah. And Priya admitted that she may have seen *something*, but she was sure it was only a reflection or maybe a refraction of light. I asked her if she smelled him, and she looked at me with such deep concern that I dropped that line of inquiry.

Four days later, a water taxi driver leaned over the side of his boat during low tide and saw my sister's body below him. In the great sorrow of that day, I lost my sense of caution and I pressed the matter again with Priya, asking what exactly she thought she'd seen that night. She snapped, "This is crazy. You think it was your childhood monster? It was nothing."

But I'd recognized the long arms and the wing-like flaps and the sidling, confident movement. I know that I'd caught, once more, a glimpse of what it is that comes to take us away.

*

For years, the cloak of grief held me under its damp, pressing weight, and the only time I ever felt alert was in the archives at the library or deep in the world of a book. Talking to Priya or my parents or the throngs of school children I was expected to usher through the library collection was like interacting through muslin. I studied every detail of Hannah's drowning, turning my memory of it inside out. Not only the what-ifs of what might have happened if I'd jumped in or the unanswerable questions around what caused the fall, but also how high the moon was, how fraught the sea. How the leafless bushes had held onto their winterberries. How the staccato thump of the waves against the seawall resembled the trapdoors in our arteries opening and closing. I tried to recall precisely that peculiar dusky smell and the way the air thickened and cracked open and the feeling that bloomed in my chest the moment I knew Hannah had passed through. This is all I can tell you. Like all stories about death, you're left with the survivor's incomplete tale.

Only recently have I been able to lend my attention more fully to the details of the present world. And I notice, sometimes, just before I fall asleep or when the motion-activated lights in the library archive go out, a certain flicker of movement and then a feeling of airlessness. And it's like, if I didn't want to, I wouldn't have to breathe. And I wonder why the connection that passed between Hannah and me all our lives, which was the pride of our bohemian mother and the unease of our cautious father and as normal to us as eating or drinking—would be severed by death. In the darkness, I open myself up. I become what I am meant to be: her mooring on the other side of all that smoke.

Deserving of You

Tabby and Ann-Marie have been best friends for twenty-nine years, since they were assigned seats next to each other in the first grade. Tabby is a hairdresser, the only daughter of Polish Jews who own a barbershop. Ann-Marie is a cognitive psychologist and professor at Yale University, the only daughter of a stern father who makes lenses for telescopes and a mother who died when Ann-Marie was four. They hail from the same tiny Western Massachusetts town, which Tabby misses desperately and Ann-Marie talks about with bemused disdain, the way one might describe an embarrassing ex-lover. They now live in West Haven, Connecticut, in separate houses, though not too long ago they were roommates in a cramped converted cottage whose backyard opened onto the Long Island Sound.

The two women and Paul, Ann-Marie's fiancé, are spending the weekend in Sandwich, Massachusetts, staying at the summer home of one of Paul's colleagues. All three of them are drunk after a late dinner that was made later by a long wait and incredibly slow service, which Paul and Tabby found hilarious and Ann-Marie was deeply annoyed by. The house looks like the centerfold of a nautical-themed home-decorating magazine, and the women have had a good laugh at the ships in bottles, the "Gone Fishin'" sign in the kitchen, and the gloomy paintings of lighthouses surrounded by swirling white-capped waves.

Tabby pulls a Scrabble box from under the coffee table and the bottom flaps open, spilling tiles. She and Paul break into giggles. Tabby begins cleaning up and notices Paul wince as he drops to his bad knee to help. He is ten years their senior, already a widower.

"This trip was just what I needed," Tabby says from the floor. "You guys are so good to me." Tabby leans her head onto Paul's shoulder.

Paul clumsily puts a hand on Tabby's thigh and pats it. "We all take care of each other."

"I know this is a hard time for you," Ann-Marie says. "But you always land on your feet. If there is one thing that can be said about you, it's that."

"I know," Tabby says, worrying the edge of the Scrabble box. Tabby is having a crisis of confidence, brought on by her thirty-fifth birthday and the impending loss of her job. The owner of the salon she works at is moving and closing shop. Ann-Marie wanted to cheer Tabby up, and the trip has, at least temporarily, done just that. While Tabby has been cheerful and glad to be at the beach with her friends, Ann-Marie is the one who's been sullen all day, stressing over a grant proposal and put off by the traffic and the biting flies and the heat.

"I didn't mean to bring up the bad news," Ann-Marie says. "I'm sorry."

"Oh no. I was just thinking. Not moping." Tabby gets a new bottle of wine from the kitchen. "Actually, it's not *necessarily* bad news. I suppose it depends what I decide."

"Why are you being so cryptic?" Ann-Marie asks.

"Craig asked me to move to Boston with him in the fall. He wants me to be a partner with him when he opens his new salon."

"That could be amazing," Ann-Marie says, suspicious as always. "What's the catch?"

"I'm not sure I'll do it."

"But if Craig's serious about opening the shop *with* you, that's a big deal."

"It is. Or it could be, if I decide that's what I want." Craig's the best boss she's ever had. But Tabby feels the walls closing in on her when she thinks of saying yes, or when she thinks of saying no.

"We'll miss you," Paul says.

"Ann-Marie and I have never lived more than five miles apart," Tabby says. "Except for the six months I tried college."

"So I've heard."

"I moved into her dorm when I dropped out."

"I know."

"I thought her roommate was going to kill me that first week. I set up shop in the dorm bathroom and cut all the Harvard brats' hair. I made a killing. I thought I was rich."

"You weren't paying rent," Paul reminds her.

"She was like a celebrity after the first month," Ann-Marie says. "The week before graduation she was booked solid. The TA for my statistics class asked me to stay after once because she was getting married and had somehow heard about Tabby's styling prowess."

"I remember that. I was all the rage. Though, really, I was more like a curiosity act."

"That's not true. Why would you say that?"

"It *is* true. Just because you really loved me doesn't mean all those other kids did. I was a fad."

"You always sell yourself short," Ann-Marie says.

"But the point is, if I move to Boston, we'll break our streak."

"Maybe I'll move with you."

"That would be difficult to explain to your clamoring grad students and your department chair."

"I'd commute."

"And your fiancé?"

"He'd understand," Ann-Marie says.

"I'm very understanding," Paul agrees.

Tabby takes Ann-Marie's hand. "I don't know if I'm going, really." She turns to Paul. "Is it weird that this is hard for us, two grown women?"

"Yes." Paul nods solemnly.

"You're kidding now," Tabby says. "But when you first started coming around you were so uncomfortable with the fact that we were living together and still so close."

"It just made me feel old. When I was your age I'd already been married for five years. Laura had already been diagnosed."

"This is a big decision," Ann-Marie says, cutting Paul off. She hates hearing anything about his late wife. She prefers to think her lovers have no romantic pasts, which fascinates Tabby, who always wants to know everything. "When does Craig want his answer by?"

"Soon. I want to talk to my parents first. About maybe taking over their shop."

"You'd really move back to Deerfield? What would you do there? Join your mother's book club?"

"They read some great books in that book club," Tabby says. "Do not insult the book club. And I'd hate to see their shop close."

"Me too. It's the only part of Deerfield I have any real attachment to." Ann-Marie turns to Paul. "When we were kids, I spent more time in the front window of that barbershop than I did at my dad's house. I would read or do my homework while Tabby styled my hair."

"Why didn't you ever learn to cut hair?" Paul asks.

"It's not in my blood," Ann-Marie says.

"It's a calling, not a choice," Tabby says, and she can see that Paul doesn't understand that she's joking.

"One day I want to meet your parents," he says, peering up at Tabby. He's still sitting on the floor among the spilled Scrabble tiles.

"You'd like them," Tabby says. She feels the intensity of his gaze and worries that she might blush, which makes her blush. She busies herself pouring more wine. Ann-Marie shoots Paul a look when he lets Tabby refill his glass to the rim, but he either doesn't notice or pretends not to.

"I used to worship her parents," Ann-Marie says. "They're like Tabby—very lovable."

Tabby gestures to the Scrabble board and asks whether they should start a game. But Ann-Marie is supposed to let the fish for tomorrow's dinner marinate overnight, and she insists that she has to prepare it now. Tabby and Paul urge her to forget about it. But Tabby knows Ann-Marie is always faithful to her to-do lists, even when she is exhausted and tipsy and on vacation.

Tabby moves to the floor next to Paul so they can set up the Scrabble board.

"Do you think she's upset at us?" Paul asks. "For drinking so much?"

"Probably," Tabby says. "But she'll feel guilty about being mad in the morning." Tabby knows that Ann-Marie is worried about living with Paul. She thinks Paul will realize how difficult she can be. And Ann-Marie *can* be hard to live with. She's demanding and high strung, because she has her plans—her very good plans—and she hates to deviate. Tabby has learned to walk the minefields of Anne-Marie's moods. Paul will learn, too, because it's worth it.

Paul plays a nonsense word with all seven of his Scrabble letters, and Tabby follows suit. They play in silence until Tabby connects GORAT to SARTEX, and Paul pushes her tiles away.

"GORRAT has two R's," he says.

"No," Tabby says. "You're thinking of the British spelling."

"I really will miss you if you leave," Paul says.

"You thought you were getting a package deal," Tabby teases. "Two pretty women."

"I like our little threesome," he says.

"You should have met some of Ann-Marie's earlier men." Tabby pulls a face. "Boring or crazy. No one deserving of her, and no one I'd want to be tied to for the rest of my life."

"You think I deserve her?"

"Of course I do," Tabby says.

Tabby is not self-deluding. She knows she's jealous of Ann-Marie and Paul's relationship: their uncomplicated intimacy and their private jokes and the way his arm fits comfortably but not possessively around Ann-Marie. She is also, she supposes, jealous of Paul, since he's slowly replacing the precarious role she plays in Ann-Marie's life. After thirty, best friends are supposed to move into the periphery; she has always been at the center of Ann-Marie's world. And maybe there's also the fact that

Paul is very attractive—hitting his stride now, at forty-five, confident while still carrying a boyishness that she suspects was needy and unattractive in his early adulthood. Every so often, in moments like this one, glancing sideways at his unassuming face, Tabby's stomach flips. She's ashamed of how much she likes the heat where their legs are touching.

"You don't think I'm too old for her?" Paul asks.

"At first, maybe," Tabby admits. "But no one our age could keep up with her. I like that you're not intimidated by her."

"She is intimidating," Paul says proudly. "Dauntless."

"That's a good word for her. The perfect word, actually." Tabby has always admired how Ann-Marie carves her place in the world and wrangles her life into the shape she wants it. Ann-Marie uses some inscrutable formula to decide who and what she desires, and latches on without letting go.

"You're *both* so talented," Paul says. "It's amazing. It's amazing that you've let me into your lives."

Ann-Marie comes into the room, happy and self-satisfied, as she always is in the moments just after completing a task. She stops abruptly halfway to the couch.

"Our chef is back," Tabby says loudly, shifting her knee.

"With all her fingers," Paul says.

"I'm done with the fish. But the wine has gone to my head. I think it's time for us to call it a night."

"It's still early," Tabby says. "We're on vacation this weekend." She raises her glass.

"I'm exhausted, Tabby."

Paul moves to get up and wavers, landing back on the floor. He rubs his bad knee, as if it is the culprit instead of the wine. Ann-Marie waves a hand at him. "Don't let me ruin the fun," she says. "You guys stay up."

Paul looks nervously around the room. "Sweetheart, come sit with me."

"When we lived together, you never went to bed before two," Tabby says. "You can't have aged that much already."

"It's been a long day. I'll see you in the morning." Without waiting for a response, she turns to leave the room. Ann-Marie was never a morning person. In grad school she would sometimes still be on her laptop at the kitchen table when Tabby came down to make coffee. Ann-Marie would stay up a while longer and they would chat until Tabby was fully awake and Ann-Marie was relaxed enough for bed.

Paul looks around the room again, as if looking for an escape route. "Do you think she's angry?"

"Yes." Tabby stretches her sunburned legs out over their game. She pushes down on them so white lines the shape of her fingers appear and then disappear. "It's not just us," Tabby says. "She's worried about that grant."

"You're probably right," Paul says. "But of course she'll get it."

"Of course. But she thinks if she stops obsessing for one second, everything she's worked so hard for will suddenly vanish."

"Sometimes it drives me a little crazy," Paul confesses.

"How could it not?"

"So will you take that job and leave us both behind?"

"I'm not being cagey. I'm not like Ann-Marie—I don't know exactly what I want all the time. When I first left Deerfield, I thought it was such a miracle to live in a place where things stayed open past eight p.m. and I could walk down the street without everyone I passed knowing who I went to prom with. But now that doesn't seem so important. And I can't remember why I was so afraid of becoming like all the mothers in that town. They were happy, or happy enough."

"That's just what Ann-Marie is still so afraid of," Paul says. "Being unexceptional."

"Yes, but she's an Ivy League professor. And I cut hair."

"Nonsense," Paul says. "There are many ways to be remarkable."

Tabby asks Paul to tell her about his first wife. She knows almost nothing about her, because Ann-Marie knows almost nothing about her, except that she and Paul were high school sweethearts and she died of some slow-moving cancer. "Losing Laura didn't make it hard to still be a doctor?"

Paul laughs. "I'm a podiatrist. It didn't make cutting old people's toenails any harder."

"Yes, but all that time in hospitals."

"It made *everything* harder, for a while. But not my job, specifically."

"Poor Paul. And you never complain." Tabby rests her hand on his knee. He puts his hand on top of hers.

"I've been luckier than I have any right to be."

"Me too," Tabby says. "We have that in common."

"Perhaps this is a horrible thought, but sometimes I think it's easier to be a widower than a divorcée. My friends who're divorced don't seem to recover. The way I mostly have."

"You do have a lot of divorced friends," Tabby says. "Is it a doctor thing?"

"Want me to set you up?"

"Not with those old fogies."

"Very nice," he says. "Do I fit in that category yet?"

Tabby studies him and pretends to consider. "You are looking pretty beat. You've got one hell of a five o'clock shadow."

Paul runs his hand across his face. "So I do. Disgusting."

Tabby snorts, and puts her fingers against his cheek. It's steel-wool scratchy. "It's not a good look for you."

"What am I going to do about it?"

"You're talking to a barber's daughter."

"Did you really used to shave customers?"

"Sometimes," Tabby says. "The shop's appeal was that it was like an old-timey barber shop. So we did shaves."

"One second," Paul says, rising unsteadily to his feet. "Don't move."

Tabby thinks that probably she should go to bed. She's in one of her moods. When he comes back, she'll suggest they call it a night.

Paul returns holding his shaving cream, a hand towel, and an old three-blade razor. She would have taken him for an electric razor man.

"I was kidding."

"So you're all talk. Not up for the challenge?" He plops down on the couch. "Well, okay. I don't want to end up with gashes all over my face. Or shaving cream all over Dr. Stephen's impeccable furniture."

Tabby holds her hand out in front of her. "I'm steady as a rock."

"Very impressive. So?"

Tabby goes to the kitchen and retrieves a bowl of water and another hand towel. She sets the bowl of water on the coffee table and spreads the shaving cream on her palm.

"Now we're talking," Paul says.

Tabby drops a knee onto his thigh to get down to his level—the couch is low to the ground—and runs the shaving cream over his face. He closes his eyes. It's too late to stop whatever this is, even if she wanted to. She leans his head back and keeps one hand on the side of his face to steady him. "Relax your jaw," she says. "Stop biting down." She tilts his head to a new angle and runs her thumb through the small bit of dark hair that falls over his forehead. Paul scratches his ear with his left hand, which is shaking. The tableau they make is weird and intimate, and Tabby feels closer to him than she's felt to a man in a long time.

When she finishes, she wipes his face clean with one of the towels and uses his chin to angle his face to all sides to examine her handiwork. Paul really is a beautiful man. Tabby thinks it's a shame that there's no good vocabulary for telling a man that he's beautiful. She thinks it's a shame that she's done. She knows she wants him, but almost abstractly, the way she might want something from a dream before she's fully awake and the rest of the world comes into focus.

"All finished," she says.

"Not even a nick," he says.

"Was there any doubt?"

"Not any," he says as he pulls her towards him. Tabby hasn't been kissed this way—full of slow desire, unashamed but not greedy—in years. Tabby's other knee lands in between Paul's legs, so she is still slightly above him, and her hair forms a curtain around their faces. He smells like shaving cream and tastes like wine plus something sweet. His cheeks are as smooth as polished stone. Her fingers curl into his hair and pull slightly. The kiss doesn't build—neither of them moves their heads—but it lasts. Tabby places one hand on his lap, over his erection, and holds it there. He moves forward slightly, but that is all. Tabby climbs off him and sits on the other side of the couch.

"We can't," she says, even though she knows he's also already decided this.

"I'm sorry," Paul says. "That was stupid."

"Really stupid. Colossally stupid."

"I know. Let's please just forget the whole thing."

"This, or anything like this, is never going to happen again," Tabby says. "I love Ann-Marie more than I could ever love you."

"Me too," Paul says, surprised and a little annoyed. "Of course."

Tabby puts her face in her hands. "I'm horrible."

"No," Paul says. "I'm the one."

"You can never tell Ann-Marie." Tabby feels suddenly sober, as if a rush of cold air has swooped into the room and returned her firmly to earth.

"It wasn't anything. No harm done," Paul says, though he can't possibly believe that.

"Let's just sit here for one more minute," Tabby says. "And then go to bed."

When they gather their nerves and stand up, Paul says, "Tabby, I am a middle-aged, soon-to-be twice-married podiatrist. There are not a lot of opportunities for me to do profoundly stupid things, and I was never one to do stupid things when I had the chance." Tabby doesn't know whether he intends this to be a justification or an apology, or both.

"Good night, Paul," she says.

After she settles into bed, Tabby thinks, it was just a kiss. Just one kiss. But Tabby suspects that in some ways this is worse. If they had started anything more, clumsily pawing at clothes and guessing at what the other wanted, it probably would have ended not only in regret and guilt but also in disappointment. Instead, she already longs for the moment back, a little spring coiling inside her as she calls up the memory. Perhaps the best course of action would be to tell Ann-Marie about the kiss, as a joke, making it a tiny, insignificant thing, something so harmless it's not even worth hiding. But Ann-Marie is jealous and insecure, for all her outward self-assurance. She can never know. Tabby hopes Paul doesn't become confessional in the morning—tears and a big to-do. She can't quite picture the outcome: Ann-Marie screaming and slamming doors and stomping among the carefully placed sea glass and dried starfish, then screeching away in the car? Ann-Marie is not the screaming and stomping type.

Tabby wakes early. Her mouth is dry and sour and a headache is pulsing behind her right eye. She wishes she could talk to Paul before he does anything stupid. He's not accustomed to making mistakes, so perhaps he doesn't know that the best way to clean up afterwards is to march onward and not look back. If nothing bad comes from it, it's not a mistake. Tabby gets dressed, finds Paul's keys, and drives to the store. She has the living room all cleaned up and a batch of pancakes warming in the oven before Paul and Ann-Marie emerge.

When Paul wanders into the kitchen and sees Tabby, he looks so unsure and guilty that Tabby wants to smack him.

"You cooked for us," Ann-Marie says. She pours herself and Paul coffee. Paul sits down at the table and puts a napkin in his lap, as if they're at a restaurant. Does he always eat his meals like that? Tabby can't recall.

"I thought the smell of pancakes might be the only way I'd get you up before noon."

"I'm not like that anymore," Ann-Marie says.

"News to me." Tabby brings the pancakes to the table.

As they eat, they talk about their plans for the day—visiting the glass museum and the Sandy Neck lighthouse, coming back to grill the fish Ann-Marie prepared. Paul finally admits to his hangover, as if this was some big revelation, and the women roll their eyes. Tabby talks about George, the big Maine Coon cat she and Ann-Marie shared, and how he used to patrol the beach until dusk.

Tabby can see that Ann-Marie is trying too hard to act normally. Maybe Paul did tell her after all. But then he wouldn't be so nervous. Tabby finally decides that Ann-Marie is upset about the moment she witnessed before slinking off to bed, or she simply senses that things have changed between Paul and Tabby.

Paul brings the dishes to the sink, but as soon as he turns the water on, he puts a hand on his temple and massages it. "I think I need to go lie down," he says. "I can't handle my alcohol anymore—not that I ever really could. You two can drink me under the table."

Ann-Marie watches him go, her fingers wrapped around her coffee mug in a tight grip, as if she will squeeze it into shards. When they hear the door shut, Ann-Marie says, "I'm going to ask you something, and you need to answer me honestly."

"What's up?" Tabby asks.

"Is there something going on between you and Paul?"

"He's your fiancé. There's nothing going on."

"Not even interest? On either of your parts?"

"What's brought this on? Paul loves you. And you, darling, are the great love of my life." Tabby has long suspected that Ann-Marie can read her mind—she is always answering questions Tabby hasn't spoken aloud or bringing up subjects Tabby is thinking about. And how could she be so confident—confident enough to make these outrageous accusations?

Ann-Marie studies her coffee with great interest. Her eyelashes, long even without mascara, shade her half-closed eyes. Without looking up, she says, "If there was something going on, I would have to choose one of you."

"Don't even say that," Tabby says, trying to keep her voice light. "Don't even think it."

"But it's true. You know it's true."

"If you want me to stop teasing Paul so much, I will. But this is how we've always been with each other's partners. You are an unrelenting flirt with every man I date. At least with the ones you approve of."

"I do not flirt," Ann-Marie says, just the smallest hint of emphasis on the 'I.'

"Not with the men you date," Tabby says. "But with all my partners you do. Remember José Miguel, your senior year? I thought you were going to steal him from me for sure."

Ann-Marie doesn't even smile.

"I'm teasing, come on."

"I've left room for Paul to screw up in my expectations for him," Ann-Marie says. "But that's not what I expect from you."

"Hangovers always make you so dramatic," Tabby says.

"Paul told me." Ann-Marie gets up and leans against the counter, as if she can't stand to even be close to Tabby. Tabby watches Ann-Marie from behind the dark shadow of her headache. Above Anne-Marie is a framed plaque with Sandwich's seal and motto, *Post Tot Naufragia Portus*. Yesterday, Ann-Marie had translated for them: "After so many shipwrecks, a haven."

Finally, Tabby says, "So that means he told you it was nothing. Nothing *at all.*"

Ann-Marie doesn't answer.

"Okay, so if you feel like you have to choose, choose me," Tabby says, mustering the last sliver of glibness she has left in her.

Ann-Marie throws her coffee cup into the sink, and Tabby is at least glad for a reaction. "Fuck you, Tabby," Ann-Marie says. "We already sent out our wedding invitations."

"Of course *that*'s what matters most to you." Tabby laughs. Ann-Marie never publically admits defeat. "You'd already chosen him anyway," Tabby says, and the truth of these words floods her with sorrow.

"You made a mess of *everything*. And you made my life into a joke."

"Wait," Tabby says. Her mind is moving too slowly. She needs it to wake up. Talking her way out of messes of her own creation is Tabby's specialty. "What if we just decided not to let it be a big deal? We have always made our own rules."

"You haven't even apologized, Tabby."

"I'm so sorry. You can't even imagine how sorry I am."

"I can't stay here," Ann-Marie says. She takes the seasoned fish out of the fridge and dumps it in the trash. The sudden smell of ammonia turns Tabby's stomach. "I'm packing. You can finish cleaning up."

*

The morning is unusually clear and the drive home feels cinematic, but it belongs in a different, happier movie than the one they're living. As they make their way towards the highway, Tabby studies the cottages adorned with colorful buoys, the ocean blue and scintillating as it spreads away from the land, a heron flapping its clumsy wings. A little girl with her snub-nose pressed against the window of her own car stares at Tabby with a look of wonder, perhaps amazed at the novelty of seeing an adult in the back seat.

It isn't until they pass into Connecticut that the full weight of the morning hits Tabby and turns her body heavy and soggy with despair. She imagines the boundary between the states as sharp and visible, chiseled into the earth. Tabby tries to console herself by thinking that the separation with Ann-Marie was always going to happen, was already happening. After being so close for so long, could she really be satisfied with only the scraps of Ann-Marie's love and attention? Tabby decides she'll call Craig as soon as she's home. She'll take the job.

Tabby hears Ann-Marie shift positions in the front seat and realizes that there's no music playing. The car is silent. They've been almost preternaturally still. It reminds Tabby of holding her breath during a game of hide-and-seek. And Tabby *would* like to trick the universe into losing sight of them, so they can have this last car ride together, pretending they are still one unit, one unconventional family. She wishes Paul would continue down the coast, following the highway for as far as it will take them. She'd like it if the car ride would never end. But of course, when their exit comes, he takes it.

Sarah Lane's School for Girls

I have told this story many times, but I have always told the simple version, which is to say I have always told it wrong. The version that I tell is this: when I was a sophomore in high school at a girls' boarding school in Vermont, the dean's sixteen-year-old son fell through the ice and drowned in the lake near campus. I tell people about the wave of morbid excitement that rippled through the hallways of our dormitories. I tell people that the event had a profound effect on me even though I'd only spoken to John a handful of times, and I let people draw their own conclusions as to why that might be. Maybe people assume it was an early eye-opening experience that proved death can be brutal and doesn't always spare the young. Maybe they interpret it as a quiet woman's desire to relive melodrama or nostalgia for the peculiar comfort one feels after a communal tragedy.

All of the above is true, but it doesn't do the story justice. Although I always hope it will, telling the sound-bite version doesn't make me feel any better or get me closer to the answers I want. If nothing else, after all these years I'd like to finally get the story right.

*

The buildings at Sarah Lane's were mostly in the style of Georgian Revival—solemn red brick with side-gables and neat rows of windows. A high stone wall surrounded the campus on three sides, with woods on the fourth, and beyond that, a lake. Though the gates were always left open, we rarely left campus. Howland, Vermont didn't have much to offer us, except for a video rental store, an ice cream shop, and teenage boys we never had the guts to talk to anyway. We did our work and were mostly polite to our teachers, and we had enough fun living with one another instead of our parents that we didn't complain much, even in the oppressive stillness of the long Vermont winters.

I wound up at Sarah Lane's on a scholarship that the school put in place to smooth over tensions with the locals. My guidance counselor had told my mother I was a likely candidate, and for the rest of eighth grade Mom insisted on helping me finish science projects and essays. She was a night nurse and my father was an electrician whom she had never married, and her daughter would be going to school with the children of politicians and lawyers. It was 1994 and the Clintons had just entered Chelsea at Sidwell Friends. My mother joked that we were following suit. I was worried that the other girls would recognize me as an outsider right away, so I spent my freshman year watching and listening, keeping my head down. I only visited my parents on holidays, even though they both lived less than twenty minutes down the road.

At the start of my second year, I realized that I'd overcorrected and blended in too well. Everyone liked me well enough, but only because I kept my mouth shut and didn't take sides. The thrill of being at a new school and the fear of failure that had kept me sharp started to wear away. By December I was crawling out of my skin, desperate for a break from the monotony. Then John disappeared and shook us all out of our routines.

Most of the girls at Sarah Lane's barely knew John, but we were intensely curious about him. He was a junior at Howland High, the town's public school. We'd watch him eating dinner at the faculty table in the dining hall with his father, whose dark hair and broad shoulders he'd inherited. Occasionally he'd catch us staring at him and flash a crooked smile. Giggling, we'd turn away before his father noticed. We were all terrified of Dean Anderson, whose mission in life was to scare teenage girls into becoming serious, respectable women. The dean was enormous, with sunken eyes and a close-lipped smile that never seemed genuine. His right leg dragged behind him slightly when he walked, which gave his movements an air of deliberateness and added to the impression that every move he made was calculated. Dean Anderson's wife had died when John was a baby, and we shuddered when we talked about John trapped alone in the dean's house with only his austere father for company.

*

Susannah Wayland, whose uncle was a policeman in Burlington, was the first to hear about John's disappearance. At the start of geometry, she whispered the news to Missy Davis, who asked Mrs. Conway whether or not it was true. Our teacher reluctantly confirmed the rumor, but asked us to keep quiet about it until more information became available. By third period, it seemed like every girl at the school had heard about the dean's missing son. In chemistry, I tried to catch the eye of my roommate, Nicky, and was surprised to find that she was still and silent, staring down at her notebook. I'd seen Nicky alone with John several times, but whenever I'd asked her about it, she'd skirted the subject with an abruptness that only increased my curiosity.

Nicky had been my roommate since freshman year, and after a week of living together she'd anointed me her best friend. She always gave off the impression of barely contained energy, even in the dead of winter when the rest of us were tired, beat-down, and settled into our routines. She snuck off campus on mysterious trips and never got caught. She had a secret stash of cigarettes that replenished itself without explanation. She spoke to our teachers with a boldness that would've gotten most of us suspended, but for Nicky there never seemed to be any consequences. At least part of Nicky's immunity came from the fact that her family was the type of wealthy I'd thought only existed on television shows or in countries with noble bloodlines. But Nicky was a force in her own right, impossible to oppose.

Nicky was also our resident authority on everything grotesque. Friday evenings, she occasionally gathered us at the stone fireplace in the student lounge and regaled us with urban legends that thrilled us and left us unable to sleep. So when the rumors about John escalated and we began to talk about death instead of disappearance, everyone wanted to bring their theories and questions to Nicky.

*

Late that afternoon there was a meeting in our dorm room to discuss what we'd heard. Eight of the girls from our hall squeezed together on the rug in between Nicky's bed and my own. Outside our window thick streaks of snow were falling.

John and his father had been seen walking into the woods before dinner on Tuesday—two days ago—and only the dean had returned home. The dean had called the police after John missed dinner. In the early hours of Wednesday morning, a search party found John's blue parka hanging on a tree branch next to the lake. About twelve feet away from the bank there was a large hole in the ice. And that was all we knew.

Every girl had her own theory, and we were divided. The less imaginative girls suggested it had been a terrible accident; John, in his recklessness, had tested his luck on the ice and fallen in. Sarah Johnston was the first to mention suicide. She pointed out that only a fool would have believed the ice was safe this early in what had been an unseasonably warm winter. Laura Parks leaned in close to the center of the circle and whispered that with a father like Dean Anderson, suicide might make sense. I suggested that it was possible John wasn't dead. What if he'd staged his disappearance? Why would he leave his parka hanging there like some morbid place marker if it was just an accident? Swayed by this romantic possibility, several girls changed allegiances. Our debate continued as dusk fell, and then night. We talked through dinner and study hall, distributing granola bars and care-package cookies instead of trudging to the dining hall.

It was almost ten when Nicky finally spoke up. "You're all wrong," she said, and the group grew silent. Our room was dark now; only my small desk lamp shone in the corner. Nicky's eyes darted across our faces, and her mussed blonde hair reflected the lamplight. "It was murder." Just then Ms. Tiggs, our dorm monitor, burst into our room, eliciting shrieks that peeled into laughter. She shooed everyone out, muttering about how we shouldn't be enjoying ourselves when tragedy had struck so close to home. She glared at Nicky but did not admonish her.

As we prepared for bed I asked Nicky if she really believed what she'd said.

"It couldn't be suicide, and I don't think he would run away either. He wasn't reckless. He was stupidly safe. He would've known not to go on the ice."

"Be honest with me, Nicky," I said, studying her. "Were you and John dating?"

"We were lovers," Nicky said, as if this was the first time I'd asked, as if she would have always answered so frankly, as if this was a normal sentence for a sixteen-year-old girl to utter.

"But who would hurt him?" I asked. "Why would anyone want him dead?"

Nicky made a funny sound like a giggle. I realized she was crying. I stood near her awkwardly, hoping she'd give a sign of what she expected from me. I rested my hand on her shoulder, feeling the bounce of her sobs.

*

When I woke the next morning Nicky was already dressed, applying mascara in front of our full-length mirror.

"We're going to investigate," Nicky said, somehow sensing that I was awake.

"Investigate what?"

"John's disappearance."

"That's not our job," I said.

"Really, Emily? John's *missing*. Who cares whose job it is?" Nicky locked eyes with me in the mirror without turning around.

"But where would we even begin?"

"I think his father killed him."

I laughed. "You have to be kidding."

"John told me stories. Dean Anderson's as terrible as a person can be. He used to hit John. I saw the bruises. No one knew because the dean always hit him where his clothes would cover it. He'd wince sometimes when I touched him."

I couldn't believe it, but I also didn't understand why Nicky would make the story up.

She sat down on the edge of my bed. "If you think I'd lie about this, then you don't know me at all."

"I believe you. But you have to admit it's a pretty wild theory."

"That's why we're going to investigate." Then she laid out her plan. During the all-school meeting, we'd sneak out to the lake. It was almost a mile away, and I wondered what would happen if we got caught rooting around the place John had last been seen.

Nicky hopped off my bed and went back to the mirror. "Get dressed," she said, and I didn't ask any more questions.

*

School meeting usually consisted of announcements about clubs and weekend trips, but that Friday the meeting began with a speech from the police chief. We were told to cooperate if anyone asked us questions, show sympathy to the dean, and support one another. As he spoke, Nicky fidgeted, pumping her leg so hard I could feel the vibrations in my own seat. John's body still hadn't been recovered, the chief said. Tripping over his words, he explained that John's body could have drifted to any part of the lake. The hole was already beginning to ice over again. He implored anyone who had information about the incident to come forward. Every part of me was burning to tell the chief what I knew; I would've felt the urge to help him even if I didn't have pressing information to share. That was just how I was then—how I probably still am. Nicky put her lips against my ear and hissed, "Let's go."

She pulled me from my seat and put her arm over my shoulder, angling me toward her, as if I was crying. The other girls, bored with the chief's rambling speech, watched enviously as Nicky led me down the aisle. Once we were outside Nicky reached out and zipped up my coat. It was an uncharacteristically tender gesture, almost maternal. I followed her to the edge of the woods. The sky was already growing dim and a steady snow had started to fall. A walking path snaked through the woods to the lake, but the snow had rendered the path nearly unrecognizable.

"Are you going to tell the police that you and John were dating?" I asked as we wound through the trees.

"They'd just tell Dean Anderson. And I don't want to answer all their stupid questions."

"Don't you think you need to tell them what you know?"

"Things aren't that simple, obviously."

I didn't want to admit that I couldn't understand why it wasn't simple, so I let the matter drop. My snow-covered hair stuck in clumps to my face and water dripped through the collar of my coat. After a while I said, "The dean is a lot bigger than John."

"So you think he would have fallen through the ice, too."

"Yes."

"I already thought about that. He could have held John under the water and then swum back, climbing onto the thicker ice by the edge. But probably he killed John in some other way, and made the hole himself, then left the jacket for the police to find. John wouldn't have drowned otherwise. It's not like he couldn't swim."

"What if he hit his head or something? Or got hypothermia. I read somewhere that it only takes a few minutes."

"You've already made up your mind," Nicky said.

"Haven't you?"

She shook her head, the ice in her hair knocking together. "I think either the dean killed him or he ran away. Maybe he's just laying low somewhere, waiting until the police go away so he can contact me."

I stared at the back of Nicky's legs as we hurried forward, trying to keep my balance and avoid missteps. The snow had turned into icy rain and I could barely see. The trees twisted and swayed around us. Everything seemed to be moving. I looked down and discovered that my right hand had been cut and was bleeding. My clothes stuck to my body. I yelled for Nicky to slow down. She turned to face me and said something I couldn't hear. A streak of mascara stained one cheek, and her face was pallid from the cold. She darted away and I stumbled, losing sight of her.

I wondered if I'd be able to follow my footprints all the way back to campus or if they'd been erased by the storm. I knew Nicky would be furious with me if I turned around. I pushed on, until suddenly the white plain of the lake spread before me. It was smaller than I remembered. Ripped police tape dangled from a nearby tree. I imagined Dean Anderson, lumbering through the dark pines.

There was a rustling to my right, and only a dozen or so yards away there was a body hunched over by a tree, clawing at the snow. I screamed. The figure rose and turned to me and before I could flee I saw it was Nicky. She was smiling and holding a small wooden box in her hand.

"It's John's. He wouldn't have left it if he'd run away. Or there'd be a note for me."

"We came all the way out here for that tiny box?" I tried to curl and uncurl my frozen toes.

"I didn't know what we'd find," Nicky said.

"We need to get back to the dorms right now. It's late—they're going to notice we're gone. We're going to get into so much trouble."

"That's not going to happen."

"Not to you, maybe. Not everyone's so lucky."

Nicky gestured towards the lake. "You call this lucky?"

"I'm serious," I said. "If we get caught, I could lose my scholarship. We need to go *now*."

We ran, stumbling through the snow, the entire way home. I never looked back, terrified that I'd see someone chasing us. I don't know what I was expecting—a menacing stranger, the lumbering Dean, or John's bloated corpse. Even after we'd finally fled the woods, I still felt that there was something sinister at our heels.

*

Back in our room, wrapped in my comforter and rubbing the feeling back into my feet, I demanded that Nicky show me what was in the box. She took out a few sheets of folded paper: poems and notes written in a meticulous hand. But she never lingered long enough on any of them for me to read more than a few words. We changed quickly and Nicky helped me wash and bandage the gash on my hand. Then we rushed to make an appearance in the dining hall. The other girls kept asking us where we'd been and why we were flushed. "We don't feel well," Nicky told them. "We had to rest."

Sarah Rodriguez gave us the update on everything we'd missed. Other girls now suspected Dean Anderson, and someone had posited the theory that John and Mrs. Mullen, a young English teacher, had been having an affair. When Nicky left the table to get tea, the other girls asked me if she'd said anything about John. I said she was taking his disappearance pretty hard.

"Some girls are starting to talk about *her*," Laura Parks said, her eyes wide and innocent.

"What're they saying?"

"That they've seen her with John. That she's always leaving campus, and—"

Nicky returned with an extra cup of tea for me, and we all studied our food.

"I hope you're not coming down with anything, Nicky," Laura said. "Especially so close to midterms."

"How can you possibly think about midterms right now?" Nicky shook her head. "A person has disappeared, and is maybe *dead*. It's ridiculous to worry about exams."

The rest of us sheepishly agreed with her, but we knew that the drama of John's disappearance wasn't going to stop the gears of Sarah Lane's from turning for long. Our commitments were waiting, and we of the never-missed deadlines, of the always prepared, would be ready to meet them.

*

The next day, while Nicky was in her cello lesson, I turned our room upside down. John's box was tucked inside a dirty shirt in her hamper. The poems and notes were packed inside two layers of Ziplock bags. So there was some echo of his father's deliberateness in John. Many of the poems were dedicated to or about Nicky, and most were a little angsty and brooding, but there was nothing about abuse or his dad.

That evening I confronted her. "You've got to give me a better reason not to go to the police."

"They wouldn't believe me," she said.

"Maybe that's because you're wrong."

"Dean Anderson is a lonely, perverse man and I know that he did it. I *feel* that he did it. He acts so calm and put-together all the time, but there's a reason everyone tiptoes around him."

"What if they ask me how you knew John? I'm not going to lie to the police."

"Are you threatening me?"

"Of course not. But you're asking a lot. If you really think the dean is involved, we have an obligation to say something."

"What about our obligation to figure out the truth? To *make sure* there's justice for John."

"You're not thinking clearly, Nicky."

"If the dean ever found out we accused him, he'd try to have us expelled."

The prospect of returning to my mother's house a failure, surrendering the promise of a Sarah Lane's future, was impossible to consider. "Okay. I'll keep quiet about it. For now."

"I knew that's all it would take to convince you," Nicky said. "I just had to get you thinking about yourself."

"I've done so much for *you*. I nearly froze to death yesterday," I said.

"John probably did freeze to death!"

"Lower your voice," I hissed. People could probably hear Nicky through the thin walls. If the girls were talking about her, they might be talking about me, too. The realization made me nervous, but it was also exhilarating.

"Listen. John and I were at the lake last week and I walked onto it—just a few feet in," Nicky said. "It was completely solid at the edges. But John wouldn't even take one step onto the ice and begged me to come back to land."

"You need to tell someone this."

"I'm telling *you*."

"That's not enough. This is a big deal."

"He loved me," Nicky said, her eyes filling with tears. When I reached out to her, she gripped my hand so hard it hurt. "We need to go to John's house."

"What are we going to find there that the police haven't already uncovered?"

"There might be *something*. John wrote everything down." She put her arms around my neck and held me. "Please," she said. "You're my best friend. I don't trust anyone but you."

*

Nicky planned our next trip more carefully to ensure that our absence wouldn't be noticed. I was to go through the week like nothing was wrong and arrange for us to have lunch at my mother's house on Sunday.

That Wednesday, as I was leaving my English class, I ran into the dean. I smiled and edged past him, but he asked if I had a moment to talk. I hadn't had a full conversation with Dean Anderson since my first semester at the school. I moved to the side of the hallway, but he said it would be better if we went to his office. He led me out of Hartley Hall and across the snowy lawn.

In his office, he motioned for me to sit. The room was uncomfortably warm; an old steam radiator ticked in the corner. He took a long time to settle down, pulling off his leather gloves and laying them carefully on the desk, unwinding his scarf and hanging it with his jacket on an ornate coatrack. He eased into his chair with a pained expression.

"The leg gets worse with the cold," he explained. His eyes were circled by purple shadows, and there was a small red cut under his chin where he must have nicked himself shaving. I wouldn't have trusted a display of dishevelment from a man like Dean Anderson, but these small signs of grief seemed genuine and moving.

"I'm sure you want to know why I asked you in here," the dean said. "And I'm not going to keep you in agony. I wanted to check in with you about your roommate, Nicky."

I nodded and tried to remain as impassive as possible.

"She must be going through a very difficult time right now. I know how close she and John were and how devastated she is, though she isn't showing it. The last time I spoke with her, she mentioned that you'd been helping her and keeping her company through this ordeal."

"I'm doing what I can," I said. Nicky hadn't mentioned any check-ins with the dean, or that the dean knew about her and John.

"That's good," the dean said. "That's what's important—that Nicky is taken care of. Perhaps she should go home for a little while, or begin seeing a counselor."

I shook my head. "I think she's very upset, but she's coping."

"Good. She's not exactly fragile, is she?" The dean paused. "Emily, I need you to tell me the truth. I hope that you understand the gravity of the situation. My son is missing. I'm not accusing Nicky of lying, but Nicky is under a lot of stress right now, so she might not be in the best place to be...forthcoming."

"I'm not sure what you're asking."

"Has Nicky said anything to you about what she believes may have happened to John?"

I forced myself to count to three and looked up to my right. "I really can't think of anything. She *wishes* she knew what happened."

"John might have said something to her in private."

"About what?" A knot had formed in my throat.

The dean suddenly pushed his chair back from the desk so it screeched against the floor. "You're doing extraordinarily well here, Emily. You don't take this place for granted. You realize what an opportunity you've been given and you take advantage of it."

"Thank you, sir."

"Does it surprise you that my background is much more similar to yours than it is to Nicky's? You're here entirely because you're smart and you *earned* a spot. Not many of the other girls can claim that. You also, I imagine, have a little more perspective."

I nodded.

"So you know what the stakes are. Can you tell me what Nicky told the police?"

"She didn't talk to the police," I said. "I mean, I don't think she did. None of the other girls know about her and John, at least not for sure, if that's what you're asking."

"I didn't think you girls kept many secrets from one another. I guess she's always held herself a little apart." The dean glanced at his watch and then turned to look at the windows, which were foggy with condensation. "It's nice that she found a friend like you, especially with everything she's been going through, on top of missing John."

I didn't want to take the bait, but I couldn't resist. "What other things?"

The dean snapped his eyes away from the window and studied me. He let out a long, exaggerated breath, as if I was forcing information from him. "I assume you already know that Nicky is pregnant."

After a long pause, I said, "That's ridiculous."

"Not ridiculous," the dean said. "Sad, perhaps. John told me several days before he went missing."

"Do the police know?"

"I haven't told them. If Nicky wants to, that's her decision. I don't see that it would change much, except the way people think of my son."

"Nicky doesn't think he ran away," I said. "Or that he drowned on purpose."

"You will understand when I say I take small comfort in that."

"But if John was afraid of what might happen—or didn't want to be a dad? Maybe he did run."

"I raised John better than that," the dean said. "You may go, Emily. If you think of anything, I hope that you'll come to me right away. My door is always open to you."

I nodded and got up. I needed air. "What if Nicky needs help?" I asked. "With the baby?"

"I don't think that Nicky's family requires assistance from anyone."

As much as I wanted to flee the room, there was one more question that had been bothering me. "Why do you think John left his coat on the tree?"

The dean shrugged. "We'd walked almost a mile. I'd taken my jacket off, too." His answer sapped all the magic and promise from the detail, which I'd hoped would be the key to the mystery. I regretted asking.

*

On Sunday morning, my mother picked us up in her twelve-year-old hatchback, her too-red hair pulled into a tight knot. She talked the whole way home, telling me about my uncle's messy divorce and her best friend's new job. She asked me questions about my classes and the quality of the dining hall food. I must have answered, though I have no memory of what I said. I was worried about what Nicky would make of my childhood home, a duplex in a row of houses that were nearly identical. I was afraid Nicky would be appalled at the place's size and shabbiness. Or maybe the house wasn't run-down enough, and it would belie my image as the resilient scholarship kid, climbing out of squalor.

When we arrived, Nicky took in the living room's faded rug, the chunky Dollar Store candles on the mantle, and the yellowed curtains and declared the place "cozy." As we sat on the overstuffed sofa and sipped Diet Cokes, I was surprised by how easily Nicky and my mother fell into conversation. Nicky asked my mom about the stack of library books on the coffee table, about growing up in Vermont, about her Christmas plans. I couldn't understand how Nicky was so calm, considering the risk we'd be taking in just a few hours.

After Nicky told my mother about the new wing of the school library, my mother confessed how much she would have loved Sarah Lane's.

Nicky asked where my mother had gone to college. I hoped Mom would give Nicky the short version, but Nicky got the full explanation. My mother, valedictorian of her high school, was the first in her family to attend college. She'd started at the University of Vermont, in the honors college, but had become pregnant with me the summer after her sophomore year. She'd left the university and gone for her nursing degree at a community college while we lived with my grandparents.

"Were you scared when you found out you were pregnant?" Nicky asked her.

My mom considered. "I must have been. But mostly I remember being so angry. At myself, of course." She looked at me, but I couldn't read her expression. I wonder, now, whether this is the closest I've ever come to an explanation of why my mother decided to keep me. She wasn't religious or conservative, but she had high expectations for herself, and perhaps felt she deserved to face the consequences of not meeting them.

After a lunch of chili and grilled cheese sandwiches, my mom drove us back to school. She put her hand on my arm and waited for Nicky to climb out of the car before asking, in a low voice, "Why'd you really want to come home?"

"I was homesick," I said.

"Are you in trouble?" Mom asked. "You can tell me if you are."

I swore I wasn't.

"This is the best place for you," Mom said. "Don't mess it up."

"I really miss you," I said, surprising us both.

She hugged me, and I climbed out of the car.

*

After Mom was out of sight, I wanted only to return to my dorm and curl up in bed with whatever book I was supposed to be reading for English class. But Nicky was already ushering me forward, informing me that we only had an hour before the dean came back from his after-church errands. I didn't know what to say as we made our way to his house. Something felt different between us. Nicky filled the silence.

"You know, the dean's limp isn't real. John told me the leg was injured in a car accident, but it healed. The dean didn't stop limping because he liked the affectation."

"That can't be true."

"Why are you still defending him? This is how he gets away with everything. You think because he's a dean, he's too *respectable*. No one wants to break the Sarah Lane's spell."

"What do you mean?"

"You know. The myth that this place is perfect, that it's better than everywhere else."

"It *is* better," I said.

Nicky sighed and her breath made a cloud in the cold. "I guess you really believe that."

The back door was unlocked when we arrived, as Nicky had said it would be. The house was small but stately, with vines hugging the brick and thick-paned bay windows. Inside, there was a stale, damp scent I normally associated with basements. We were silent as we crept upstairs, as if the house might collapse on us at the slightest noise.

John's room was in complete disorder. Clothes and books on the floor, lights knocked over, sheets in a clump at the foot of the bed. Nicky picked up a Walkman and turned it over in her hands, looking more like an archeologist exhuming ancient artifacts than a detective gathering evidence. She sat down on John's bed and put her head in her hands. She stayed like that until the silence made me squirm.

"I know," I said finally. "About the baby."

Nicky lifted her eyes to me and then narrowed them.

"The dean knows, too," I said. "John told him."

"And then the dean told *you*?"

"He wanted to find out if I knew anything. I told him I didn't."

"This changes everything. *That's* his motive. He has a horrible temper, and if John finally told him . . ." Nicky began to rock back and forth. "How could you hide that from me?"

"You hid a pregnancy from me. You hid a *relationship* from me."

"I wanted to tell you."

"I would have helped you, if you'd trusted me."

Nicky shook her head. "You don't understand. I'm starting to think you'll never understand. You always do whatever's expected of you, as if that's the only option."

"I don't have other options. Not everyone gets to make mistakes and stay on top. I shouldn't even be here right now."

"Then why did you come?" Nicky asked.

I had no answer.

Nicky pulled a folded piece of paper from her pocket and held it out to me. It was a letter from John—short and focused, unlike his moody, abstract song lyrics. In it, he said he couldn't understand how she was considering keeping the baby. He insisted he loved her—he'd loved her their whole relationship and loved her now and would love her no matter what happened. But his father would be furious when he found out. Nicky pointed to a sentence, underlined twice: "He'll kill me."

"Now do you believe me?" she asked.

"Nicky, *this,*" I said, shaking the letter, "is evidence. We need to give it to the police."

"You're not on my side anymore," Nicky said. "If you ever were." She stood up and kicked at the mess on the floor. She ripped the blanket off John's bed. I tried to quiet her, but she scrambled back onto John's mattress and screamed into his pillow. In the presence of her fury, I only felt embarrassed.

The sound of tires outside finally quieted her. We listened for a moment, then raced to the hall. We could've made it. We could have run through the front door and been free, but we stood, paralyzed, until it was too late. We heard the slow twist of the door handle. Nicky took one step toward the stairs before spinning around and nearly knocking me over. We stumbled back into John's room. A door slammed; keys clinked onto a table. Nicky threw open the window. A burst of cold air blew her hair away from her face. She swung her legs up and climbed on the ledge.

"Don't," I hissed. But she'd already jumped. The footsteps downstairs stopped. I ran into John's closet, hiding myself behind the clothes. There was a baseball bat leaning against the back wall. I picked it up.

"John?" the dean called weakly. I heard his footsteps pounding up the stairs. A man with his limp could never move like that. Just before he rounded the corner I slipped out of the closet and opened the bedroom door.

I thought that if I surprised the dean I'd be able to see in an instant what he knew, whether he'd witnessed the accident or even caused it. But his face revealed nothing. He recovered his composure before I could even speak, pushing past me into John's room.

"Nicky!" he roared.

"She's not here," I said.

"Where is she?" He opened the closet.

"This was my idea."

He turned to me, chest heaving. "Don't lie to me, Emily. You are not in a position to lie."

I still had the note Nicky had shown me balled in my fist. I smoothed it out and handed it to him. "Nicky showed this to me last night, and I thought you should have it. I was going to leave it for you, anonymously. I don't know what I was thinking, coming upstairs. I was just curious."

The dean read the note. The paper shook in his hand. "This is a serious violation. You won't be coming back from this, I'm afraid. You must know that."

I put one hand on the doorframe. My mother's chili rose to the back of my throat and burned.

"Maybe," the dean said, folding the note, "if you tell me where Nicky is and admit that she brought you here, I could help. If you tell the truth, the repercussions won't be as severe."

"Okay," I said. "This was Nicky's idea. I don't know why she wanted to come, I swear. But she left, a while ago. I came back alone." I tried to think about what a real Sarah Lane's girl would say to shake herself free of consequences. "I wonder," I said, and then stopped because my mouth was so dry I needed several tries to swallow. "I wonder if my being here might look pretty bad for you, too. I mean. That I knew how to get inside your house? That we were here alone, together?"

"You're not very good at threats," the dean said. "If that's what that was."

"I gave you the letter from John," I said. "*Please.*"

We watched each other until I could hardly bear the silence. The dean nodded. "Get out."

"Thank you," I said, close to tears. "I'm so sorry. Thank you."

"You are done playing detective, Emily. There will be no more chances."

I turned and fled down the stairs and out into the street, taking in big gulps of the fresh cold air. When I reached an intersection, I stopped to get my breath and heard footsteps crunching across the snowmelt. I whipped around and saw Nicky running towards me. She had been waiting for me all that time.

*

We didn't talk until we were back in our room. I leaned against the door, my heart racing. Nicky clutched her right hand to her chest.

"What happened?" she demanded. "How did you get out without the dean seeing?"

"I didn't," I said. "He found me." I told her the excuse I'd invented and about my ill-formed threat. I thought Nicky would be impressed.

"You gave him the letter?" she said. "*My* letter?"

"I had to give him something. He was going to throw me out of school. You still don't get it—I can't just shake consequences off with one call home to Daddy. I didn't have a choice."

"God. That's just like you. Of course you had a choice. That letter was our proof. And it wasn't yours to give."

"You almost ruined my life and now you're angry at *me*?"

"You're proud of yourself, aren't you? For weaseling your way out of trouble. He's going to destroy that letter, or use it in the wrong way—

twist it around into something it's not. You're a coward. You think that Sarah Lane's will somehow make you matter, or make you matter more than everyone else. But it won't. You're a small person, carving yourself off from everything that might make you less small."

"You're a hypocrite. You would've given in, too." As soon as I said it, I knew I was wrong. Nicky navigated the world by her own set of inscrutable rules; she didn't compromise.

Nicky climbed into bed, still holding her wrist. Days later, when she finally went to see the nurse, we learned she'd sprained it in the fall from the window. Soon after, we found out the baby hadn't survived.

*

Nicky and I never told the police about the pregnancy or the dean's knowledge of it. In retrospect it seems bizarre and almost wicked that we withheld so much information, not only about the pregnancy but also about Nicky and John's entire relationship. The mystery of John's death was never solved. His body, or what was left of it, was found in April when the ice thawed enough for a proper search. For months I kept myself awake at night, imagining that John's ghost would return, furious that I hadn't told his story. I continued to speculate, always considering some new perverse explanation. Maybe, once John was alone, egged on by Nicky's accusation that he was too tame, John stepped onto the ice. When the spiderweb of cracks spread underneath his feet, he would have realized it was too late. Still, he'd have turned to the shore and taken one long stride toward his hanging parka before sinking, forever, into the slime of the lake. Or, perhaps, he was trying to escape the heavy future that suddenly loomed before him, in the only way his adolescent mind could see how. And I suppose it's not impossible that Nicky was right to blame the dean.

Nicky never quite recovered. Soon, all the girls knew about her failed pregnancy, although they never confirmed whom the father was. Nicky kept John's secret, just as the dean suspected she would. The girls' envy quickly turned to pity; Nicky's brashness—her unapologetic rule breaking—became an object of ridicule instead of admiration. Nicky was pregnant again by the time I was a junior in college at Wellesley. Once I'd elbowed my way in, I never left the small, protected world of academia. I finished third in my class and, after graduate work at Harvard, secured a job as an American studies professor at Emerson. Nicky and I fell, mostly, out of touch.

The last time I spoke with Nicky I was a senior in college, up late one Friday night working on my thesis. Nicky called, frantic and sobbing, demanding to know why I hadn't gone to the police. Why hadn't I told the truth? Her voice dripped with anger. From the way her words ran together I could tell she'd been drinking.

"He's still out there, Emily. He's still there."

"Who is? John?"

"Dean Anderson. He never got what he deserved. That bastard. That complete and utter bastard. He took everything from me." On the other end of the line I heard a loud knocking and a man's muffled voice.

"It was just an accident, Nicky," I said with more confidence than I felt.

"You are so full of shit." Nicky paused for such a long time that I thought she'd hung up. "No—it's not that at all. You're empty. You never felt *anything.* You just knew things. You knew that they would never discover the truth, and you knew that I was going to lose everything. I thought you might have had the courage to be on my side."

"I *was* on your side." I paused to think about it, to remember. "I was."

"If that helps you sleep, you can believe it."

Nicky hung up before I could respond. The air in my dorm room seemed to be buzzing with electrical charge. Nicky had not lost her dramatic flair, nor her ability to leave me with fresh doubt, dread, and excitement. I pushed aside my books and went to the window. It was later than I'd realized. I watched girls stumbling back from parties, happy and comfortable in each other's company.

*

I think I understand now why we didn't go to the police. My world, my new and superior world, couldn't have remained intact if the dean was hiding such a hideous secret. And Nicky needed the dean, the embodiment of all that had not protected her, to be guilty. So we kept silent, tolerating a mystery that allowed both of us to go on living in the worlds we had constructed for ourselves.

I still dream about John. In my dreams Nicky and I weave through a snowy forest, with trees that writhe and thrash on every side of us. Although he never speaks, sometimes the dean is there, slinking through the shadows at the edges of my vision. We reach the lake and John is waiting. He hangs up his blue parka and turns. Nicky runs to stop him, but he pushes her aside. John dances onto the ice and Nicky follows him. The ice begins to split and groan beneath their weight. The dean appears at my side while I watch, and I feel his enormous hand on my shoulder. Then the ice cracks open with a noise like thunder. As Nicky lunges to save him, John casually sidesteps the fissure. As she plunges into the water, Nicky reaches out to me for help, but I am frozen and I cannot move.

Four Houses Down

We'd been living in the house on Black Brook Road for two months when I heard the howling coming from down the street. It was storming that night, as it did all that August, and the cries had to rise above the noise from the wind and the angry trees and the rain. The howls came every minute or so, each one a sob that would break open into a scream. The sound was so strange and so wild that when the first shriek woke me I was sure I was dreaming it.

I was twelve that summer, starting the sixth grade in a month, and I liked to think of myself as tough. I never cried, I wore boys' jeans, and I practiced defiant stares in the mirror when I got out of the shower. But the noise that cut through that windswept night filled my mouth with a sour taste and made my heart thump loud in my chest. I rolled onto my back and listened, watching the shadows that the shuddering tree branches threw onto my walls. I heard my sister's footsteps flap across the hallway and then she slipped into my room.

"Do you hear that?" Katrina whispered when she saw I was awake. She kneeled near the edge of my bed, her long hair mussed from sleep. She was fifteen and trying to look out for me. "What do you think it is? Wolves?"

"There aren't any wolves here," I said, sitting up. We had moved one town over from our last house, less than ten miles, but our new street was flanked with deep woods and it felt isolated, belonging to a different type of small New England town. I cocked my head and listened for the next scream. "It's a woman, definitely."

"That's even worse," Katrina said. "I've never heard anything like it."

I got up and walked to the window, placing my forehead against the cool glass. The road was slick with water and the lamplight jumped across the pavement as the rain fell. I moved to the far edge of the window to increase my range of sight. The lights were on at Miss Browning's, four houses down on the other side of the street. Another shriek filled the night and my head bumped the glass. Katrina squealed, but softly enough that our father wouldn't know that we were awake. He had taken to sleeping with the television on, and we could hear the drone of voices through the wall. "It's Miss Browning, I think," I said. "The lady with the cats."

"What's wrong with her?" Katrina asked. "Someone should help."

I glanced over my shoulder and rolled my eyes. "Are you volunteering?" I wondered if other people on the street were pushed up against their own dark windows. Although my family was still on the outside of it, the neighborhood was tightknit. It pulsed, breathed like one being. It was the kind of place where the kids played hockey in the street, built forts in each other's yards, and had sleepovers whenever permitted. Whatever was happening at Miss Browning's would become part of the street's undercurrent of gossip. If I asked the right people I knew I could solve this mystery.

"I heard that she's crazy," Katrina said. She wouldn't come stand with me, as if just being near the window would put her in danger. "That's what Alex said about her, anyway."

"Alex is always making stuff up." Alex Wilson and his two brothers were key players in our street's band of kids, and Alex presented himself as an authority on all neighborhood matters. I suspected most of what he said was grossly exaggerated, but our next-door neighbor, Mrs. Haycock, had also warned me about Miss Browning. She'd told me to stay out of Miss Browning's yard and not to pet the cats that lived there, because Miss Browning was a "private" person. There was an army of half-feral cats that prowled the woods behind Miss Browning's. Most of them were all white, with one blue eye and one yellow eye. They had shriveled ears and long, mean faces.

The howling slowed and eventually stopped. I climbed back into bed. Trina scooted in next to me, pulling the covers up to our chins.

"This place is too weird," she said. "I wish we were home."

"What's the difference? We barely moved."

"Emma." Trina flopped onto her side to face me. "You can't be serious. You *grew up* in that house."

"There's nothing wrong with this house." I said. "And, as an added bonus, it seems we live down the street from a werewolf now."

"I don't buy this little tough guy act of yours for a second. There's no way you're happy about having to go to a different school. You must miss Mansfield."

"I don't really care one way or the other."

"Liar." She squeezed my stomach playfully and I pushed her hand away.

"You don't know how I feel."

"Relax, I'm only teasing. *I* miss home, anyway."

"You just don't want to be away from Brian," I said. Katrina was in the process of mourning, publicly and loudly, the loss of her boyfriend, a floppy-haired skateboarder. He'd found the prospect of their long-distance relationship too challenging.

"So what if I miss him?" Katrina rested her head against my shoulder. "One day you'll understand," she said, as if she were wise and world-weary for pining over a boy who'd once said he thought dinosaurs were mythical creatures, like unicorns.

After a few quiet minutes, Katrina got out of bed. She surprised me by kissing me on the forehead. I snapped my head back. She asked, "Are you going to be okay alone tonight?"

"Knock it off, Trina. I'm going to be fine."

But after she left I couldn't fall back asleep. I couldn't stop thinking about Miss Browning's wailing: the wildness of her sobs, the unapologetic way she'd forced her suffering outwards onto the night. When I finally slept I dreamt of her odd-eyed cats, spitting and yowling in the tree outside my window.

*

I woke the next morning still preoccupied with thoughts of Miss Browning. My father was surprised to see me downstairs so early as he got ready for work. I asked him if he'd heard anything last night, and he said that he hadn't.

"Why, what'd you hear?"

"Nothing—just that the storm was bad," I said.

"Was it bothering you? You can tell me if you're having trouble sleeping." His concern embarrassed me. He was always trying to catch me at odd points in our conversation, wanting me to admit to emotions I wasn't feeling.

"No, I *like* storms."

"All right," he said. "But the rain's cleared up now. You should spend some time outside. Maybe actually talk to the other kids. If the Wilson boys are playing basketball, you should join them." He picked up his bag and headed toward the door, stopping with one foot in the house and one foot out. "And don't go easy on them, either. Take them for all they're worth."

Since we'd moved to New Coventry, I'd spent most of my days reading or playing basketball in the driveway by myself. I'd also been exploring the woods on the other side of the street. I was using sticks and old boards to build a small fort, and occasionally I'd find strange treasures to collect—sea glass, marbles, an action figure of some off-brand hero, a toy mouse, a plastic ring. I didn't spend much time with the other kids, which bothered my father, who'd chosen the house partially because he liked the way everyone in the neighborhood got along. The other kids seemed fine, but they didn't interest me.

I knew my dad was worried about me. A year and a half earlier my mother had died in a car accident, swerving on the highway to avoid a crashed motorcycle. She was in the hospital for two days, but she never woke up. I had spent my time since then steering my thoughts away from her absence, trying to outrun the wave of sadness that trailed behind me. That summer I was just starting to resurface, finding that I didn't have to be so protective of my thoughts, which wouldn't wander quite so quickly to darker places during moments of stillness. I felt like I was climbing out of a murky body of water and the world was clearing again, taking on crisp outlines that I hadn't realized were missing. It was a bad time to come to my senses and reenter the world—the last few weeks of summer were sunless and dank. It stormed during the nights and a slow drizzle fell almost every day. The drizzle wasn't enough to drive me inside, but it got underneath my skin so that I never felt dry. It was a summer of soggy socks, squeaking shoes, and toes that blistered and swelled.

I was emerging from my grief into a feeling of invincible boredom and a new persona: defiant, brave, untouchable. The world had done the unthinkable to me. What other threat could it possibly pose? The new school, the new town, the drafty house that my father spent his evenings and weekends repairing—they were all just changes in scenery. But Miss Browning was something to fix my thoughts on. I wanted to know more about her. She was a strange-looking woman, but she had a shadow of prettiness about her, like a beautiful building in decay. She was tall and slim, her face angled and sharp. She had coarse, slate gray hair that she wore in a long braid. It was hard to guess her age, but I assumed around seventy. I'd heard her house was full of junk. Her backyard was crowded with odd refuse: an old washing machine, wheelbarrows, a rocking horse, dozens of birdhouses. The kids in the neighborhood said Miss Browning performed weird rituals in the shed behind her house, which was why the door was always padlocked.

Before Katrina woke up, I slipped out to the woods and looped around to Miss Browning's property. When I neared the shed in the back of her yard, I thought I heard something moving inside. I walked to the wall and put my ear against the shingled siding. There was definitely someone in there. It sounded like someone was dragging something heavy, or scraping something away. There were no windows on the shed. I slid to my knees and cupped my hand over my ear so I could hear better. After a minute I heard feet sloshing through the spongy grass and leapt to my feet.

"What the hell are you doing?" Katrina hissed, her face splotchy with red. She was in her pajamas, and without her makeup she looked years younger, like an old picture of herself. She dragged me towards the woods instead of angling back across the lawn.

"We don't have to hide," I said. "I wasn't doing anything wrong."

"Like hell you weren't. And that woman is *nuts.*" Katrina yanked me down the path until we were hidden by the trees.

"Calm down. I was just curious."

"Hoarders are *mentally ill,*" Katrina said. "She is clearly severely unbalanced."

Miss Browning had never seemed sinister to me, only odd. I liked the pale blue of her eyes and I liked that she kept to herself. When I had run into her in the woods, she'd given me a half-smile that seemed genuine, lacking the put-on cheerfulness that adults reserve for their interactions with children. One of the white cats had been following at her heels.

Katrina dragged me home and made me promise that I wouldn't go back, warned me to mind my own stupid business or she'd tell Dad what I was doing, and stormed upstairs to shower. I just barely stopped myself from shouting up to her that she wasn't my mother.

*

Over the next few days I pieced together more of Miss Browning's story, mining information from Mrs. Haycock, who'd lived in the neighborhood for forty years and whose own kids were grown and gone. She babysat for the younger kids on the street and had her hand in everyone's business. Although Katrina and I insisted we were way too old for babysitters, Mrs. Haycock made dinner for us every Tuesday and Thursday, when my dad taught his evening seminar.

From Mrs. Haycock, I learned that Miss Browning had grown up in the same house that she now lived in. She'd inherited it from her parents. As a child, she'd been a talented ice skater, even performing nationally. She'd been competitive, popular, and smart. But as she grew older she became witchy and eccentric, not liking to leave the house very often, spending all of her time painting and writing in journals. She had worked, for a time, at the veterinary clinic at the university. She never went to college, never married. But in her mid-fifties, she met Mr. Wallace, a sociable man who owned a deli in town and who'd been a selectman. He had moved in with Miss Browning after his retirement. Mr. Wallace had already been married once and had two grown children. No one understood this new match, but the couple had been inseparable until Mr. Wallace fell ill. He'd died five years earlier.

From the Wilson boys I learned that the shrieking happened once a year, on the anniversary of Mr. Wallace's death: August thirteenth. Every year the boys would wait up, huddled in Alex's bedroom under a fort of blankets. They said they suspected that Miss Browning had poisoned Mr. Wallace after he threatened to leave her, and this dramatic ritual was to ease her guilty conscience. Some people thought Miss Browning had bewitched Mr. Wallace, tricked him into loving her and accepting her crazy ways. Laura and Sam Hastings, twins who lived on the other side of her house, swore that one time they saw Miss Browning leaving the woods, stooped over, carrying a heavy sack stained with blood. Whatever was in the sack was about the size of a small dog, Laura had told me, her face scrunched up in disgust, during a game of flashlight tag I'd been invited to join.

But the story that fascinated me the most was that Miss Browning was keeping the embalmed body of Mr. Wallace in the shed behind her house. The story went that Miss Browning had an uncle who worked at a funeral home in Willington, and he had restored Mr. Wallace's body especially well. Since Mr. Wallace had never officially married Miss Browning, he would have been buried next to his first wife. So Miss Browning and her uncle brought the body back to the shed, where Mr. Wallace could stay with her forever. She was, after all, a woman who kept things for too long, accumulating objects past the point of reason. And once, when the door to the shed was slightly ajar, someone—no one could remember who—had caught a glimpse of what looked like the body of a man slumped in an old rocking chair.

The other kids in the neighborhood were happy to feed my interest in the mythology surrounding the old woman. They were surprised that I suddenly had so many questions for them, but welcoming. Katrina was interested in the stories, too, but mostly because they gave her an excuse to talk to Alex, who was beginning to take her mind off Brian. I watched the way she blushed when Alex teased her or paid her some compliment. I wondered how she could do so little, in the wake of her recent heart-break, to protect herself from this new threat.

I hoped that her crush on Alex would at least make her less homesick and bring some peace between her and my father. Katrina resented Dad's decision to relocate us and his refusal to listen to her side of things. She didn't want a clean slate, the way my father and I did. Her room was plastered with photographs from our old life. A huge bulletin board hung on the wall at the foot of her bed. In the center of the bulletin board was a blown-up photo of my mother and Katrina holding hands, standing in front of our house in Mansfield. Katrina is probably five in the photo, and she's staring up at our mother with a big goofy grin. Katrina said she'd arranged it so it would be the first thing she saw when she woke up.

Aside from Katrina's room, the only other photograph of our mother displayed in the house was a framed picture of our family at Niagara Falls, which hung above my bureau. Katrina had insisted I put it up when we were unpacking. My father wouldn't talk about all the other photos that had never been unpacked after the move.

*

One afternoon, maybe two weeks after I'd heard Miss Browning's wailing, we were forced inside the Wilsons' house by a bad spell of rain. The gang was feeling antsy and cooped up and anxious to get back outside. When I steered the conversation to Miss Browning and the corpse again, Sam Hastings finally lost his patience with me.

"If you're going to keep talking about it, you need to actually *do* something," he said.

Katrina tried to get him to shut up, but it sounded enough like a dare that I was hooked. He wanted me to break into the shed that night and report back on what was really in there, whether it was haunted by Mr. Wallace's ghost or contained his embalmed body.

"Or both," Mark, the youngest Wilson, said.

Sam said there had to be a way to break in—the metal clasps that held the padlock were probably easy to pry off the doorframe. He could even lend me some of his father's tools. There were grumblings from a few kids—ones who thought I didn't understand how real or big the risk was. But there was no way I was going to back down and lose face in front of the group. And I thought I would finally get a satisfying answer, which might placate my obsession.

On the way back to our house, Katrina asked me if I was serious about breaking into the shed. It was illegal and senseless. She said I was just being reckless.

But I loved the idea of being reckless. I *wanted* to be the type of girl who would do anything and who didn't care what happened to her.

"If you insist on being such an idiot, then I'm coming with you," Katrina said. "If anything happens, Dad'll kill me. So either way I'm dead."

Knowing Katrina would be with me was enough to push away any doubts I might have had.

*

That night I waited with my ear pressed against the wall for my dad to drift to sleep. I had stashed a bag with a flashlight, a screwdriver, and a hammer underneath my bed. The rain fell in steady pellets outside. The air in my room was heavy and damp.

When I went to fetch Katrina she was already in her raincoat, chewing on her cuticles. "We'll be so fast," she said, her knee bouncing. "We'll take one look inside that shed and then we'll come straight home."

I nodded.

"It's still early, though," she said. "We should wait."

We listened for signs of wakefulness from our father's room, but only heard the television. "It's a good thing he sleeps with the TV on now," I said.

"He does it because he can't stand to be alone with his thoughts for even a second," Katrina said, her voice strong with an anger I didn't understand. "He doesn't want to think about Mom. That's why we moved, you know."

"I know."

"You do?" Katrina asked, sounding both impressed and troubled by this revelation.

"I mean, obviously."

"Well, it's messed up. It's not normal. He can't just pretend she never existed, like we can just erase her or something."

"That's not what he's doing at all," I said, because I needed to defend our father and I didn't have the words to defend his choice. But I realized Katrina was right. My dad and I were trying to mask my mother's absence with more absence, widening the hole she'd left in our lives until we couldn't see the edges of it, until it was so big that it wasn't recognizable as a hole.

Katrina looked as if she felt sorry for me. I got up and we tiptoed down the hallway, not putting on our clunky boots until we were on the porch. Once we were outside I could breathe again. I felt none of the dread that showed on Katrina's face.

"Thanks for coming with me," I said as we walked.

"You're going to owe me for this forever."

"I know."

"You don't actually think there might be a body in the shed, do you?"

"No," I admitted. I was disappointed to have to acknowledge it.

When we got to the shed, Katrina stood on lookout, watching the rear-facing windows of Miss Browning's house. I saw what Sam had meant about the padlock; the metal loops that the padlock circled through were rusted, as were the nails that held them to the wood of the doorframe. Using the screwdriver, working the edge in slowly, I was able to tear one of the plates free.

"How will we put it back?" Katrina whispered. "She'll know."

"We can hammer it back in later," I said. I laid my hand on the doorknob, the hair on my arm prickling underneath the heavy fabric of my raincoat. I pushed my wet hair out of my face and Katrina gripped the back of my coat. Slowly, I pulled the door open a crack and shined the flashlight beam into the shed.

"What do you see?"

There was so much junk that it took me a moment to fixate on anything specific. The shed was full of smooth slabs of wood, which were painted with elaborate landscapes: forest clearings and sandy dunes and snow-covered fields. On high workbenches sat rows of birdhouses, painted like miniature post offices and churches and police stations. There were small wooden statuettes of cats and people. In one corner there were dozens of hand-painted dolls with rosy cheeks and bright eyes.

"It's amazing," I said, and I could feel Katrina's grip relax. I moved so that she could peer in, shining the flashlight for her so she could take in the wonder of it. "They're pretty good."

"They're beautiful," she said, laughing. "They're actually really beautiful."

I wanted to respond, but couldn't. I was oddly moved, and impressed by the complexity of this woman's life, to which we had ascribed such an emptiness. If the shed had been better lit, it would have looked like the interior of an antique store or the window display of a toyshop around Christmas. I wished that I had brought a camera.

Katrina took a sharp breath and grabbed my arm. The flashlight beam jerked to the floor, throwing the room into darkness. Katrina tried to pull me away from the door, but I wouldn't budge.

"What?" I demanded.

"Don't look." Katrina pulled frantically at the back of my jacket, yanking so hard that I needed to grip the doorframe to keep my balance. "Come on, Olivia. We have to go."

I scanned the flashlight over the room, trying to hold the beam steady against Katrina's hysteria. When the light swept all the way to the wall I was standing against, I saw what had frightened Katrina and I swallowed a scream. It had been too close for us to notice immediately, just an arm's length away. I pulled the door open wider and took a step into the room, Katrina still gripping my jacket in a tight fist. Against the wall, to our right, the figure of a man sat stiff and upright in an old armchair. He had silver-blond hair and an uneven smile. His hands rested, palms up, in his lap.

"It's a doll," I said. "It's just a doll." But we both knew that it wasn't just a doll. It was bigger than the other dolls, carved more carefully, painted less gaudily. And it was too ugly to be a doll or a generic statue. It was too flawed. Although neither of us had ever seen Mr. Wallace, we knew that this was him. It was a doll made to look just as he had looked in his last years in Miss Browning's house, before he got really sick but after age had carved its imperfections into his features. The surface of his skin wasn't sanded smooth; it was carved to look crumpled and loose. The spaces under his eyes were hollowed out, painted a lavender-blue and finely pockmarked. His nose was too large for his face, and the tip of it was slightly bulbous. His upturned palms were painted a jaundiced shade of yellow. The fingers seemed poised to snap shut on anything that landed in their reach. His smile was what unnerved me the most. His expression was almost mischievous, as if he were hinting at a shared secret. But the expression was also unreadable, private, turned in on itself. I couldn't tell how much of this effect was intentional, but Miss Browning seemed like a skilled and dedicated artist. She had been trying to capture a specific look of his, I was sure. One that she had loved, or maybe one that had always troubled her.

I thought of all the months, or even years, that Miss Browning had spent carving such an intricately detailed structure. It would have taken so long just to paint the thing. All that time focused on the recreation of the man she would never get back in the flesh.

Katrina slowly reached out to touch the statue and I snatched her hand away.

"Don't touch him," I hissed.

I don't know how long we stood there after that, studying the mystery of this man caught between the living and the dead, trying to read his inscrutable expression. Outside the shed the rain picked up and tapped at the roof, like fingers drumming impatiently.

"She must have loved him so much," Katrina said.

"No. This is crazy. This is completely insane." My heart was knocking against my chest and my stomach felt knotted, as if someone had taken a fistful of my insides and squeezed. "Let's get out of here." I kept my eyes on Mr. Wallace as I shoved Katrina towards the doorway. I imagined him blinking to life, his textured hair turning soft and rippling in the wind.

After we left the shed I stopped and picked up the rusted lock and the nails. "Be careful," Katrina said, but I was already hammering frantically. She hushed me and reached to stay my hands. The hammer slipped against the wet metal and caught the side of my finger. I cried out more loudly than I should have.

We turned towards Miss Browning's house and then took off running, not caring that the mud was climbing up the legs of our jeans and we were leaving big, messy footprints in the lawn. When we reached the street we kept running, our boots slapping through the puddles, our lungs filling with the damp air. We locked the door behind us and stood dripping and gasping in the front hall. I resisted the temptation to drag the living room sofa to barricade the door. A barricade would not keep out the things I didn't want following me home.

Katrina went into the bathroom to change and wash up while I went into my room. I stood next to my bureau, unsure of what to do next. The image of the doll was burned into my memory. I buzzed with nervous energy, my emotions tumbling over each other until I couldn't keep them straight. I felt as if I was on the verge of remembering something I had long since forgotten, something I would keep on remembering and then forgetting for the rest of my life.

My mother had been a professor of biology. One evening a few months before her accident, she had been driving me home from a friend's house when she pulled the car over abruptly and pointed out my window at a large Victorian house. A strange swarm of dark, writhing shapes was billowing out of the attic window. "A colony of bats," my mother explained, leaning so close to me that I could smell the sour-sweet of her breath. It looked like the house was breathing black fire. Soon, the bats scattered and were gone. "The world is a weird place," my mother had said. "A pretty wonderfully weird place." And we sat in the car together for a while longer, not speaking, with the gray dusk closing in around us.

I would live the rest of my life without her. I had loved her, and now I could never have her back. How could you face the fact of that head on? How could you spend months locked in a shed with it, build a monument to it? And why would you want to live inside your memories—be enveloped by the false promise of their warmth?

I reached for the photograph of our family on the wall and ripped the cardboard backing out of the frame. I yanked out the picture and tore it into long thin strips. I let them flutter to the ground and then got into bed, turned out the light, and pulled the covers over my face.

Even though I knew Katrina would come back to me, when the door opened I still jumped.

"It's okay. It's just me," she said, her eyes wide against the dark of my room. "Are you all right?"

"I'm freaked out," I said.

"I know," Katrina said, sliding beside me. We fell silent, comforted by the familiar way the bed held each other's weight. We listened to the steady static of rain on the windows, the tremors of wet leaves in the wind, the rhythm of our sleeping neighborhood. Katrina rolled onto her side, facing away from me, and I curled up against her. The storm had left a muddy smell on our bodies, and I breathed in her scent: wild, salty, familiar. I pressed my face into the soft hair at the nape of her neck, sensing that there was something fragile in that moment, that the unselfconscious closeness I was feeling towards her wouldn't always last.

Long after I thought Katrina had drifted to sleep, she spoke. "We can't tell anyone about Mr. Wallace. Ever. Okay?"

And we didn't. We told the other kids that the shed had been filled with boring knickknacks. We made up details about broken lamps and poorly constructed birdhouses. The other kids lost interest in our story, and we could see the extreme disappointment in their faces. And we were fine with that, knowing that we owed Miss Browning the right to her private incarnation of grief, aware of how glad we were that no one could pry into our own minds and unearth our own secrets to judge them against the impossible standard of normalcy.

Later that night, when the thunder that had been threatening finally came and shook the windowpanes, Katrina and I woke next to each other and held hands, and I did not hide the fact that I was afraid. I remembered that I had torn the photograph, and with a desire so fierce it felt like being set on fire, I wanted the picture put back into one piece. I understood, then, that even with all that I had lost, I was not done losing. I understood that I was not done acquiring things worthy of being lost. I understood that love is not a thing that stays buried for long. I closed my eyes and I listened to the storm rage.

Acknowledgments

First, I want to express my extreme gratitude and appreciation for Diane Goettel and the whole team at Black Lawrence Press for bringing this collection into the world and making it the best version of itself. Diane's voicemail will be saved in my phone forever.

Thank you Zoe Norvell and Christopher Gee. I love my cover so much!

Thank you, a million times over, to the editors and readers of the magazines that published earlier versions of many of these stories.

Thank you to Taryn, Gibson, Meghan, and everyone else at the Maine Writers and Publishers Alliance. The Maine literary community is incredibly lucky to have you. I'm also grateful for the support I received from Hewnoaks Artist Residency, which kept me going and allowed me to finish this book.

I owe so much to my teachers, elementary through MFA. Shout-outs to Mrs. Higby at Ambrose Elementary; Mr. Miles, Mr. Donahue, and Ms. Swan at Winchester High School; and Paula Sharp, Charles Barber, and Sarah Carney at Wesleyan University. Special thanks to the Ohio State MFA faculty: Lee Martin, Michelle Herman, Erin McGraw, Andrew Hudgins, and Kathy Fagan. This would be a very different book without your guidance and support. Thanks, too, to Eddie Singleton for teaching me how to teach, and for always giving the best book recommendations.

To my OSU MFA classmates and dear friends, thank you for being the first readers of many of these stories, and for your astute commentary. Thanks, also, for everything I learned from reading your outstanding work, for coffee dates and breakfasts at Katalina's, for trips to Half Price Books and dancing until our feet hurt and commiserating when things were hard and celebrating when things weren't. Please move to Maine already.

Thanks and love to the friends who have provided me with endless support, and who continue to support me. Cassie, Allie, Shannon, Kate and Kerry, Megan, Val, Tiffany, Jordan, Chelsie, Jamie Lyn, Shelley, Clare and Ava, Chelsea and Ashley, the Baxter Academy humanities department circa 2020, and the team at CBHS. There are many more of you; I hope you know who you are.

Thank you to Jared and Josh, brothers extraordinaire, for never forcing me to play Ark Nova.

Thank you to my students, who remind me, over and over, why the work of learning and being curious and finding your voice is the best work there is. Thank you especially to the brave and brilliant students at Coastal Studies for Girls, my Baxter Flex Friday students, and to Turkewitz Crew at CBHS (I would've mentioned you even if you hadn't told me I needed to).

Thank you to Chelsea, the most supportive partner and best cat mom I know.

To Katie, Kristina, Meredith, Livia, and Julia, my bowling crew: you are my second family. You make my life better and easier and funnier and more joyful. One day we'll make it to that No Doubt concert.

Finally, thank you to my grandmother, my parents, and the memory of my grandfather. This book is for and because of you.